Calypso Island

CALYPSO ISLAND

by
Madge Beattie Blakey

and
Carol Collver

Illustrated by
Al Fiorentino

THE WESTMINSTER PRESS
Philadelphia

STANDARD BOOK NO. 664–32463–0

LIBRARY OF CONGRESS CATALOG CARD NO. 70–96697

BOOK DESIGN BY
DOROTHY ALDEN SMITH

PUBLISHED BY THE WESTMINSTER PRESS ®
PHILADELPHIA, PENNSYLVANIA

PRINTED IN THE UNITED STATES OF AMERICA

To
Joanne and her island friends
and
Sally, Danny, and Lynne

Contents

1

Touris' mon he come . . .

Touris' mon he come to Virgin Isle
Swim 'n' fish for jus' a little while
Peter he live here all year roun'
Wouldn't leave for all d'gold in London Town

OVER the shallow water near the shore, seabirds swung back and forth, fishing for lunch. Peter's eyes followed a dark gray pelican as it circled, hovered, then swooped down on a darting shape in the water. The bird popped to the surface and rode up and down on the gentle swells, arching its neck and throwing its head back to slip a wriggling fish down its throat. Peter chuckled to himself—everyone had to eat.

It was summer in the Virgin Islands, and Peter Van Dyke walked along the beach humming a calypso tune. The afternoon was his. Shopkeepers on St. Thomas called summertime the "off" season. There were few customers at Peter's family's shop in town. No cruise ships had dropped anchor in the harbor for over a week.

But there was nothing "off" about Peter's summers. He had the beach and the sky and the sea. And it was the sea

9

he loved best. He hurried, impatient to be in the water.

At the end of the beach the white sand gave way to rocks. Peter climbed to a place where the sea had worn a wide ledge. From this vantage point he could see for miles. As if just for him, the sea had carved a niche behind the ledge that was perfect for storing the paint box and watercolor pad he always brought with him.

He stowed his painting kit in the niche, stripped off his shirt, and ran toward the sea, his rubber fins and goggles in his hands. The cutoff blue jeans he wore were faded and frayed, but to Peter they were like a second skin—his "lucky" pants. Once a Jumbie had come to him in a dream and promised that as long as he wore his lucky pants, he would be second cousin to a fish.

His mother had given him some new maroon swimming trunks for his birthday, but he still swam in his cutoff jeans.

Peter was up to his knees in water when he remembered something. He waded back to shore and searched through the driftwood until he found just the right kind of stick— one with a sharp, pointed end.

The sea was as warm as the balmy air. Peter floated in and slipped under the surface. He swam easily, gliding by castles of pink coral and shimmering sea fans of lavender and gold.

Suddenly he saw what he was searching for—a cluster of spiny sea urchins. He swam with the pointed stick in his right hand. As he approached the purple-black, prickly creatures, he poked them with the stick, breaking spines and opening brittle shells.

He surfaced, gulped air, and returned to the sea-urchin nest. The water was alive now with rainbow-colored fish feeding on bits of sea-urchin meat. Peter watched the fish —flashing silver-blues, brilliant yellows, pinks, glittering greens, and purples. Some were marked with glistening black stripes, others were spotted.

He was so absorbed that he did not notice the thin black shadow lurking nearby. A sudden flash of fins caused him to look around quickly. His eyes opened wide. 'Cuda!

With a burst of energy he shot through the water, while all around him panic-stricken fish fled before the barracuda's dark, hungry mouth.

Peter reached shore safely, flopped on the sand at the water's edge, and rested, letting the waves lick at his feet. After a few minutes he picked up a conch shell, scooped it full of water, and carried it across the beach to the rocky ledge.

He set to work with his watercolor pad, painting the fish as they had clustered around the sea urchins. The bright colors followed his brush, and soon he was finished.

But nothing he painted ever seemed finished. No matter how hard he tried, it was no good. Maybe next time he could paint something that really looked like his world under the sea. He would try harder.

He jumped down to the beach and spread the watercolor out to dry, weighting the corners with stones. This done, he stretched out on the warm sand and closed his eyes.

Peter was almost asleep when he heard voices. He looked up. Two men were approaching.

"This is as far as we can go today, Steve," said one of the voices.

"But we don't know any more than we did yesterday. Or last week," grumbled the other.

"Take it easy," said the first voice. "We've got plenty of time."

"It's too late to do any more today," said the impatient one.

"Look," replied the first, "we're not going to find this thing overnight. Give it time. After all, it's been there almost three hundred years."

"O.K., O.K., but tomorrow let's try to do better, huh?"

"Relax, Steve. Here, put down your pack and get out the coffeepot. Let's gather some wood for a fire and make coffee."

"Wood?"

"Sure. There's some over there under that tree."

The two men had not seen Peter, and he watched them gather an armload of dry branches. They didn't look like ordinary tourists. Instead of orange- or purple-flowered shirts and silly straw hats, they wore T-shirts and khaki shorts. One was thin and tall and the other short and husky.

Peter waited until they had laid the fire. The tall one struck a match and leaned forward to light the dry palm fronds under the wood. Peter called out, "Don't do that!"

They turned and stared at him, surprised.

"Where did you come from?" the short man asked.

"And what did you say?" asked the tall fellow, whom the other had called Steve.

"I said," Peter repeated, "don't do that."

"Listen, kid, are you trying to be smart?" Steve dropped the match as it burned close to his fingers.

"Yes, what's eating you?" The stocky one was beginning to be annoyed.

"Nothing," Peter replied. "But I couldn't just lie here

12

and let you set fire to that wood."

They looked first at the pile of branches and then back at Peter.

"Why?" they asked.

"That's manchineel," Peter said. "The fruit of the tree can poison a guy."

"We don't have any fruit, just wood," said Steve.

"And we weren't going to eat anything."

"But you were going to burn it," Peter answered, "and that's almost as bad. The smoke can wreck your eyes." He watched the astonished expressions on their faces as his words sank in.

"Say, you've really done us a favor," said the shorter man. "Who are you?"

"Peter Van Dyke. I was born in St. Thomas. Lived here all my life. Are you tourists?"

"Sort of. I'm Jake Freeman," said the husky one, "and this is Steve Clark." He gestured toward his tall, thin companion.

"Hi," said Peter.

"Hello," said Steve, with just a trace of a smile.

"Well, if you're not tourists, what are you then?" Peter asked.

Steve's smile faded. "Look, kid," he said, running his hand over his straight, dark hair, "why aren't you in school?"

"School's out," Peter answered. "Didn't you know that?"

"Sure," said Jake, flashing a smile.

"And don't call me kid—please?" Peter asked.

"O.K., Pete," Jake said, still smiling.

Peter stared at him in wonder. Jake had extremely red

hair and more freckles than you could count in a week.

"How did you get all those?" Peter asked, still staring at Jake's freckles.

Jake laughed. "Say, kid—uh, Pete—you're just full of questions, aren't you? Well, I inherited the freckles—you oughta see my dad—and since you want to know if we're tourists or not, we're students and we're on vacation. Just like you."

"But you're too old to be students." Peter was puzzled.

"Jake and I are college students," Steve said. "And we're here on a, well, a research project. Get it?"

Peter felt his ears get hot. His mother often told him he asked too many questions, and now he had done it again. He hoped he hadn't hit it off wrong with Jake and Steve. They seemed like great guys, and college men too.

"I'm going to college someday," Peter told them. "I'm going to be either a painter or a marine biologist or—"

"Hold it!" Jake interrupted. "What was that again?"

"I said a painter or—"

"No kidding?" Steve broke in. "An artist?"

"Yes," Peter replied. "I come out here all the time and paint."

"Let's see," said Jake, spotting the watercolor drying on the sand.

Peter was embarrassed. It made him uncomfortable to show his work to his mother, let alone two complete strangers.

"Well, it's not much good," he said, kicking the sand with a bare toe.

"Let us decide." Jake strolled over to the picture, picked it up, and shook loose a few grains of sand. "Say," he said,

14

"take a look, Steve. We've got a budding Van Gogh in our midst."

"Got any more like these?" Steve asked, studying the watercolor.

"I guess so," Peter replied. "But they're at home."

"Could we see them?"

"Well, maybe. But don't tell anyone."

"Don't worry, Pete," Jake said. "We'll keep it between the three of us. Where can we find you?"

"I help out mornings at the Pirate's Gold shop. Grandpa Van owns it. It's next to the—"

Jake slapped his hand against a sunburned leg. "Oh, no!" He burst out laughing. "It's an omen. What more do you need, Steve?"

"What's so funny?" Peter asked. "What's funny about my Grandpa Van owning a gift shop? He's had it for years. It's sorta famous too. My dad runs it now though, and sometimes in the busy season we have—"

"That's O.K., Pete," Jake said. "It's nothing to do with you. We were feeling pretty low a few minutes ago. Now out of the blue you come up with a name like Pirate's Gold."

"What got you down?" Peter asked.

"We'll tell you one of these days," Steve replied, frowning. "But for now—"

"Oh, sure. Uh, where are you guys staying?" Peter asked, to change the subject.

"You mean where were we staying," Jake said.

"Yeah," Steve added. "We're not staying anyplace right now. We couldn't afford the hotel we were in. We may end up sleeping on the beach."

16

"Maybe you can help us." Jake scratched his head. "We don't have much money, so we're looking for someplace cheap."

Peter thought for a moment. "Mrs. Du Bois might let you have her spare room. I go to school with Alexie—Mrs. Du Bois is her mom—and sometimes she'll take people in. But not very often. She's fussy."

"Would you ask her for us?" Steve said.

"O.K., I'll try," Peter replied. "She doesn't charge much. And, mon, can she cook! Hey, is that your jeep?" he asked, pointing to the pink-and-white striped vehicle that was just like many others for rent on the island. "I hitched a ride out. If you'll drive me back to town, I'll do the best I can for you with Mrs. Du Bois."

Soon they pulled up in front of a yellow brick Danish house near the Fort.

"Wait here," Peter told Jake and Steve as he jumped from the jeep and walked toward the door.

"Hi, Peter," Alexie said, opening the screen door. "Whenyoureach?" She and Peter often talked calypso when they were alone.

"Jusnow. Listen, I've got two continentals who want a room. Nice guys. Friends of mine."

"You know my mother doesn't like boarders," Alexie replied. "She says they march all over her roses and eat everything in sight."

"I don't know about the eating, but these guys won't hurt flowers. They're busy."

"Doing what?" Alexie asked.

"They have a project. They're students."

"What kind of project?"

17

"A research project," Peter answered.

"Well, that tells me exactly nothing, stupid. You mean they're such good friends of yours, and you don't even know what their project is?"

"They're going to tell me," Peter answered.

"Going to? Like when? Oh, Peter Van Dyke, you're just showing off."

"No, I'm not. I guess I don't know them that well. But I will. And I'll bet they'll tell me what they're doing. So what about it, huh? You'll like these guys. Ask your mother if she'll take them in. They're waiting in the jeep."

Alexie leaned out of the door and squinted at Steve and Jake.

Steve looked up from a map he was studying and nodded. Jake stuck his head out of the jeep and waved both arms. "Hi!" he called.

Alexie smiled and waved back. She turned to Peter. "Well, O.K. But on one condition."

"What?"

"That you'll go with the rest of us to the party tomorrow night."

"What party? You know I hate parties."

"You won't hate this one, stupid. Guess what? It's going to be on the *Golden Goose*."

"No!" You mean that creep Vhartok is giving a party for us?"

"Wait, I haven't finished," Alexie said. "No, Vhartok isn't giving the party. That old mammeehead wouldn't do anything for us. It's his niece, Sondra."

"I didn't know he had any relatives. I thought he came out from under a rock."

Alexie laughed. "So did I. But he's got this niece. She comes into Daddy's drugstore all the time. Buys enormous bottles of perfume and gobs of makeup and stuff. Today she came in when I was helping at the counter. She invited me and the rest of the kids to this party on her uncle's yacht."

"What's she like?" Peter asked.

Alexie sighed and smoothed her long dark hair. "Oh, she's all right, I guess. You know the type."

"Hey, I'll bet you don't like her," Peter laughed. "I can always tell."

"Oh, no you can't. Now are you going to the party or not?"

"Sure. I want to get a look at this type you're talking about."

"You're hopeless. Well, I guess I'd better go ask Mother about your friends." She turned and walked quickly down the hall.

Peter waited, listening to the echo of voices coming from the back of the house.

"Mother says O.K.," Alexie told him when she returned. "Tell your friends to come on in. See you tomorrow night at seven."

"Hey, wait a minute," Peter said. "I haven't asked my folks."

"I already did," Alexie giggled, "and they said you could go."

Peter hit his hand on his forehead and groaned—women!

"Wassa serge projeck?" Jens asked his big brother at dinner.

"Jens," Mrs. Van Dyke said, "don't talk with your mouth full."

Jens gulped down his whelks and rice.

"What's a search project, Peter?" he repeated.

"Oh, Jens," Mrs. Van Dyke said, "you swallowed your food without chewing. A boy almost seven should know better. And look, you spilled food on the table again."

Very slowly, Jens put a forkful of food into his mouth. His brown eyes flashed. He rocked his head up and down and chewed, making exaggerated mouth movements.

No one paid any attention to Jens until Grandfather Van Dyke saw what his grandson was up to. Then he too began rocking his head. Peter saw what was happening and joined the chewing chorus.

Paul Van Dyke, a slender man whom Peter strongly resembled, looked up from his plate to see his two sons and his father solemnly chewing in unison. He couldn't resist joining in.

When Mrs. Van Dyke caught on, she laughed out loud.

"Oh, you're all impossible. You look like a bunch of cows chewing their cuds. I hardly think the dining room is a place for cows to eat."

Everyone laughed and went back to eating normally.

"What's a search project?" Jens asked Peter.

"You don't give up, do you?" Peter said.

"I never heard two boys ask so many questions," Mrs. Van Dyke said. "If you worked as hard answering them, you wouldn't need school at all."

"Mom," Peter said, remembering something that had puzzled him, "have you ever heard of a guy named Buddy Vango?"

20

"Who?" his mother asked.

"Buddy Vango."

"I can't imagine who that would be. Where did you hear it?"

"From those two guys I told you about. The ones staying with Mrs. Du Bois."

"Yes?"

"Well, uh, they were looking at a watercolor I did today out at Coki Bay—of a bunch of fish eating some sea eggs I smashed open. They said I was a Buddy Vango."

"I wonder what—" Peter's mother began. Suddenly she smiled. "Peter, I believe they gave you a very fine compliment."

"What do you mean?"

"It's just a guess of course, but I think what they might have said was that you were a 'budding Van Gogh.' " She pronounced "Gogh" with a little rough sound in her throat, for the "gh."

"Who?"

"Vincent van Gogh, a Dutchman. He lived and painted in France, the southeast coast mostly. Van Gogh painted many pictures using color in unusual ways. He was so different from other artists that, during his lifetime, hardly anyone understood his work. But now his paintings are considered masterpieces and sell for thousands of dollars."

Peter let out a low whistle.

"Hi, Buddy Van Coke!" said Jens.

They all burst out laughing.

The Van Dyke house was built on a hillside that rose sharply from the town of Charlotte Amalie. To get to the front door, you had to climb forty-nine steps. To get from the living room to the dining room, you had to climb some more. And to get to Jens and Peter's room, you had to go to the very top floor of the house. Here was the room the brothers shared, a room with a glass door that led to their own small patio surrounded by banana trees, white-flowered oleander bushes, and bloodred bougainvillaea.

Peter was almost asleep when he heard the noise.

Thump, thump.

"Wha—what?" he mumbled.

Thump, thump, thumpity-thump.

Peter woke up enough to realize that Jens was sending a message. They both had memorized the Morse code and at night they often "talked" to each other across the dark room.

S-O-S, Jens thumped against the side of his bed. H-I-T B-Y T-E-N B-O-M-B-S M-A-Y-D-A-Y S-O-S.

Peter answered, R-O-G-E-R C-O-M-I-N-G F-A-S-T.

G-O-I-N-G D-O-W-N, Jens thumped, S-O-S.

"Hey, Jens," Peter said aloud.

"Send it by code," Jens protested. "I'm sinking."

"It takes too long. Listen. What would you think if someone laughed when you told them about Grandpa Van owning the Pirate's Gold?"

"Did he laugh real hard?"

"Yeah. What's so funny about that?"

"I dunno," Jens answered. "Was it one of those guys today?"

"That's right—Jake. Think he was making fun of me?"

"I dunno," Jens said. "They don't sound stuck-up to me. Maybe you said something about their—their search project. Something they know 'bout and you don't. Like a secret."

"Hey," Peter said, rolling over on his back. "Maybe that's it." He lay quiet for a while, thinking. Then he called softly, "Jens, do you really suppose that's why Jake laughed?"

But Jens did not answer. Peter listened to his regular breathing and guessed he was asleep.

By now Peter was restless. He got up and went to the front window. He loved to sit there at night and watch the boats in the harbor, their lights sparkling like the stars so close overhead. Someday he hoped to paint all of that. He had tried and tried, but each time he had torn up his work in disgust.

He looked out over the sea and thought about many things he did not understand, until at last he grew drowsy and crawled back into bed and slept.

2

Old Nick Vhartok . . .

Old Nick Vhartok is very strange mon
Do a little business an' den he run
He have a little yacht only t'ree block long
An' when he fling a party it really get flung

A SLEEK MOTOR LAUNCH flying red-and-yellow flags was waiting for the party guests at the waterfront. White-uniformed sailors helped the guests aboard. The launch sped to the *Golden Goose,* Nick Vhartok's luxurious yacht anchored in the harbor.

The handsome craft was ablaze with string upon string of lights.

"Why doesn't Vhartok moor the *Golden Goose* at the waterfront?" Alexie asked Peter.

"The same reason he goes around with that stateside hat pulled down over his face. He doesn't want anyone to get a close look."

"Really? Well, why do you suppose he let his niece give this party?"

"I don't know," Peter laughed. "Maybe old Mammee-head Vhartok is human after all."

"Sh-h-h-h," Alexie warned as the launch neared the gangway leading up the side of the yacht.

A uniformed steward led Peter, Alexie, and a group of more than twenty friends and schoolmates along the deck of the yacht. They entered a passageway and were guided to the ship's lounge, where the party was to be held. When they saw what awaited them, their eyes almost popped.

"See me now, Jumbie! I dead and gone to heaven!" a voice bawled.

Peter looked around. It was Merkley Peach, the group's self-appointed clown. He had flopped down on a velvet and gold chair. His eyes were rolled up and his long, skinny arms dangled lifelessly to the floor.

"Watch out, Merk," Peter said. "Don't act too dead or you'll miss the cake and ice cream."

Merkley sat bolt upright, very much alive. He grinned broadly, revealing a wide gap between his front teeth. Merkley would do anything this side of murder to get a piece of cake.

"They no cake," he said. "They jus' pretty pink tables an' gold plates for eateen." He swept his arm in a wide gesture that took in the entire lounge.

It was dazzling. Hundreds of candles cast a golden glow over the pink satin tablecloths, gilt plates, and thin crystal goblets. The floor was waxed to a high luster so that walking on it was like gliding over ice. Across the lounge, on a raised gilt-framed bandstand, steel drums had been set up.

"Young sir," one of the stewards said, touching Peter's elbow, "would you like to take your seat?"

Peter wasn't sure what he was supposed to do. He told the steward his name and was led to a place at one of the tables. By the plate was a small card with PETER VAN DYKE written on it in gold letters.

Peter sat down, ill at ease. But he smiled and then relaxed as the steel-band members entered and took their places on the bandstand. He knew all of them and remembered what they had looked like a couple of years ago—barefoot kids, beating on their first crude drums at Lindbergh Beach. Now they played at all the best hotels.

"They look pretty good up there, don't they?" Peter whispered to Alexie, who had the chair next to him.

Before she could reply, they heard laughter at the other side of the lounge. It was Merkley again. He had picked up a fragile crystal vase of red roses and was dancing with it as though it were a girl. His feet skidded over the slick floor.

"Careful, Merk," someone called out. "Remember when Vhartok almost rubbed you out."

They tittered nervously, remembering the time during Carnival when Merkley had snatched off the stateside hat Nick Vhartok wore indoors and out. They had stared at the bald head that was revealed. Vhartok's face was deeply tanned, but his shiny head looked grayish white—the color of a shark's belly. The next thing they knew, the four dark-suited men who always stuck close to Vhartok had hustled Merkley along the waterfront by his elbows. "O.K., boys, cool it," Vhartok had barked. "Let him go. He won't try that again." His eyes had glinted with rage. He had shoved the gray felt hat down on his naked head and stalked off, surrounded by his bodyguards.

But now Merkley ignored the warnings and continued dancing with the vase of flowers. "You lookeen gow-gee-ous tonight, dahleen," he crooned to the roses, unaware of the deathly silence that had fallen over the lounge. The steel band had stopped playing.

"Now, Sweet Sugar, we tromp 'round dis way an'—"

Peter saw the collision coming. He clapped his hand over his mouth.

Merkley swung the crystal vase into the air as he pivoted, bringing it smack into Nick Vhartok's gray vest. It was as though Merkley and the vase had smashed into a cement pillar. Vhartok did not move an inch. He was rooted to the floor, his steel-gray eyes narrowed to slits.

The vase cracked and water dribbled down Nick Vhartok's immaculate suit. Merkley let go and the vase crashed to the floor.

Five years passed—or so it seemed to Peter. Slowly, color came back to Vhartok's face. His eyes flickered. He raised one arm. Merkley ducked to avoid being struck.

"Go and sit down, kid," Vhartok grunted. "This here is a party. An' I wanna tell yuh one thing. You're supposed to have a good time. Hear me? All my friends should have a good time!"

Merkley stared at Vhartok as though he had just been commanded to run himself through with a broadsword. "Yessir. Right now. Yessir!"

Merkley turned. Then he remembered the broken vase and the heap of roses on the shiny floor. As he whirled around and bent down to pick them up, his feet flew from under him and he landed smack on his stomach, the wind knocked out of him.

He gasped, raised his head a little, and looked straight at Nick Vhartok's gray suede shoes.

"Did you hurt yourself, kid?"

27

"Oh, nossir. I haveen good time. Sure am." Merkley patted the glistening floor on which he sprawled. "An' I love your pretty shiny floor. Sure do."

Vhartok turned and walked from the lounge, his body-guards trailing after him.

Peter figured that Vhartok was going to change his suit. Island rumor had it that he owned a hundred and fifty suits with shirts and ties to match and that he changed clothes from the skin out four times a day.

The door closed behind Vhartok and his crew. Merkley scrambled to his feet and pranced around, pantomiming his fall and Vhartok's stony reaction. When the door through which Vhartok had left swung out slightly, Merkley shot toward his chair so fast that his feet skated across the floor.

The lights dimmed, the spotlight came on, and into its beam walked a vision wearing a red, pink, and green sequined shirt and skintight black satin pants. It was St. Thomas' famous calypso singer, Lord Obnoxious—big bare feet, solid gold teeth, and all.

"Where's Vhartok's niece?" Peter whispered. "She's going to miss this."

"You know the type," Alexie shrugged. "She's got to make an entrance."

The spotlight followed Lord Obnoxious as he swaggered across the floor. He opened his solid gold mouth and sang, "When we eateen cake?"

At least it appeared that way.

Everyone was confused until they realized it was Merkley up to his tricks again. He had yelled out his request for cake just as Lord Obnoxious opened his mouth to sing.

The calypso singer grinned broadly. "Watch out, mon," he chanted.

They all laughed and looked at Merkley. They laughed harder as he picked up a gold plate and pretended to bite into it. Suddenly the laughter stopped.

Vhartok and his four men were marching single file into the lounge. They settled at a table apart from the rest. Vhartok snapped his fingers and the band began playing.

Lord Obnoxious improvised a song about "Mistress Sondra," their hostess. It was all about her beauty, her wit, and her many accomplishments. Alexie and the other girls fussed with their hair and looked bored.

"Here she be now
Our pretty lady-girl
Smell good like orange blossom
An' shine like ocean pearl"

The spotlight moved from Lord Obnoxious to an archway at one side of the lounge. Red velvet curtains parted and Sondra entered.

"I thought you said she was our age," Peter whispered.

"She is," Alexie said. "It's that getup that makes her look so old."

"Some getup." Peter watched Sondra pick her way across the polished floor.

In the spotlight, Sondra's metallic dress shimmered like fish scales. Her silvery blond hair was piled into a high, fluffy cloud and she carried a single red rose. She came to Peter and Alexie's table.

"I believe this is my place," she said, picking up the place card. "Yes, here I am: SONDRA FETCHING."

"She probably put the thing there herself," Alexie shot to Peter in a hoarse whisper.

"Hello," Peter said.

"Now let's see who *you* are," Sondra said, with a tinkling laugh. She read Peter's place card. " PETER VAN DYKE. My, what a forceful, strong name."

Peter felt his ears get hot. He had never heard his name spoken like that before.

Sondra perched on her chair. "Hi," she said to Alexie and quickly turned back to Peter.

"I asked Alexie if there were any cute boys on St. Thomas. She said she didn't know of any. But now I know she was wrong."

Peter felt his ears burn hotter. He couldn't think of a thing to say.

"Oh, you're not the talkative type," Sondra continued. "How perfect. I think women are naturally talkative, while men ought to be silent and strong." She laughed her tiny bell laugh again. "Don't you agree, Peter?"

"Oh—yes, sure," Peter stammered. "This is, uh, a nice party."

"But you must all be starved," Sondra said. She signaled the waiters, who brought huge platters of turkey, ham, roast beef, salads, and fruit to the tables.

After dinner the tables were removed and the chairs placed in a semicircle facing the stage. The lights dimmed and Peter saw Nick Vhartok leave the lounge, then return just before the entertainment started. His bulky outline was barely visible in the dim light.

Peter and Alexie were impressed by the entertainment. A man and woman, natives from the nearby British island

30

of Tortola, beat on bongo drums and danced. Their sequined costumes of purple and gold shimmered like sea fans underwater. She wiggled, he stomped, and everybody clapped.

Lord Obnoxious made up songs about all the boys and girls, adding hilarious comments about their latest escapades.

Peter thought his ears would burn right off his head when Lord Obnoxious sang a verse about him. He looked sheepishly at Sondra to see her eyes wide and shining as the calypso singer told about all the gold Peter made every tourist season at the Pirate's Gold shop.

He tried to change the subject. "How many knots can this ship make?" he said to Sondra.

"I couldn't say," Sondra giggled delicately. "Really want to know?"

"Sure," Peter answered.

"O.K., I'll go ask Uncle Nicky." She crossed the lounge to where her uncle sat.

Peter watched her lean over the dark figure, then draw back quickly and whirl around. When she walked into the path of the spotlight, he was surprised by her look of confusion.

"What'd he say?" Peter asked as she took her seat.

"Oh, never mind. It's a silly thing to talk about. Anyway, that man wasn't Uncle—I mean—uh, really Peter, you shouldn't ask difficult questions!"

Peter was dumbfounded. What was she talking about? He turned to Alexie, but saw that her chair was empty.

" 'Scuse me, Sondra," Peter whispered. "I'm going to the, uh, washroom. Be right back."

31

He went outside and looked around the deck. Alexie was nowhere in sight. He entered a passageway, but was stopped by a heavyset man.

"Where you going, kid?" the man challenged.

"To the washroom," he replied.

"That way." The man pointed in the opposite direction.

Peter walked onto the deck again. Still no Alexie. He was worried. This was no place for a girl to be roaming alone.

He jumped into the shadow of a lifeboat as he heard men approaching. When they passed by, Peter darted across the deck and into the forbidden passageway. The heavyset man was no longer there.

He followed the passageway until he came to a door leading down some metal stairs. He followed the stairs to another door that was halfway open. Could Alexie have wandered down here?

He pushed the door open wider and slipped into a close, stuffy room.

"Alexie, Alexie," he called in a loud whisper, groping his way along the wall. He could hardly see. The only light came from the passageway.

Peter was about to leave when he heard the rumble of deep voices. He ducked fast behind a dark, bulky object. It wouldn't do to get caught snooping around down here.

Suddenly the beam of a powerful flashlight cut a bright path above Peter's head. He inched along the wall until he found a safer hiding place in a dark corner.

Two men entered the room, talking under their breath. Peter blinked as a glaring overhead light flashed on. He could not hear what the men were saying, but caught a glimpse of one yellow pant leg.

The men left, closing the door behind them. The light still burned. Peter saw that the room was partially filled with large bamboo crates like the one that hid him. One of the crates had been pried open. He lifted the lid. Inside were four identical packages, each wrapped in a smooth, stiff material. They looked vaguely familiar.

Oh, yes, now he remembered. Last year he had helped his father unpack a crate of scrolls from Hong Kong. Each scroll had been wrapped in smooth, stiff material just like this. It was oil silk.

The stairs creaked. Someone was coming. Peter looked frantically around. There wasn't time to get to his corner hiding place. He had to get out of the room. He grabbed the doorknob and pulled hard. The door stayed tightly closed. He couldn't budge it an inch.

The footsteps sounded closer. The heavy door swung open and he jumped behind it. He held his breath, caught the doorknob as it came near, and hung on. If the door closed, he would be a sitting duck. Luckily, no one noticed that it stayed open.

Peter listened to the voices only a few feet from him. One of them sounded like Vhartok's. But that couldn't be. Vhartok was supposed to be up watching the show. Then he remembered Sondra's strange remark: *That man wasn't Uncle—*

What was going on, anyway? Through the crack at the door hinge he caught a glimpse of yellow cloth. The man with the yellow pants must have returned.

"Awright, waddya want, Whitey?" one of the voices snarled.

"More. You think you can squeeze me out, don't yuh?"

Whitey menaced. "Well, I ain't—"

"You're gettin' your cut. What's the gripe?"

"So that's all you call it. A gripe! You're making a cool five offa this deal and you say I'm griping 'cause I want my share. You dirty—"

Glass crashed. Peter winced. The overhead light went out. Peter hung on to the doorknob for dear life. He heard a sudden, heavy thump like someone falling to the floor. Now was his chance. He slipped around the door and out into the passageway. He was back in the lounge and in his chair in moments. He didn't think he had been seen.

"Where'd you disappear to?" Peter whispered to Alexie, who was in her seat at the table.

"Where were you?" Alexie answered.

"I asked first," Peter insisted.

"I got bored," Alexie replied. "Certain people I know were spreading the sugar on so thick it gave me a tooth-ache."

"Really?" Peter asked. "Which tooth?"

"Oh, never mind, stupid," Alexie said.

Girls, Peter thought. Who can figure them out?

"Watch this," Sondra said, pointing toward the stage. A limbo dancer was just beginning his act.

Peter looked toward the silhouette of Nick Vhartok. Or was it Vhartok? Just then, the man rose and left the room. Peter frowned. Why would he leave now? But no sooner had the door closed behind him than it opened again, and Vhartok returned to his chair.

The limbo dancer went into the high point of his act— or rather, the low point. The drums beat faster and faster as he inched under a bar held by two girls who lowered it

35

after each pass. He bent backward so far that it seemed his spine would crack. The drums reached a fever pitch. Sweat poured from him. Back he bent, lower and lower until the muscles stood out on his legs in hard ridges.

Then the bar was set aflame.

"Is he going to make it?" Sondra asked, wide-eyed.

"Who knows?" Peter said. They watched the quivering dancer bring his head under the flaming bar. Not a single hair was singed as he passed underneath. He leaped to his feet in triumph, executing a graceful pivot.

The group clapped with enthusiasm.

"Some party," Peter said.

"It's not over yet," Sondra said, and pointed up.

The lights came on and a hundred balloons were cut loose from the ceiling. Everyone scrambled for them, laughing and skidding on the polished floor. Alexie caught seven and won a silver bracelet with a green stone in it. One of the boys won a basketball. And Merkley Peach won a pink stuffed giraffe almost as tall as he was.

"Mon, what a party!" Peter sighed as the launch sped them back to the waterfront where Mr. Van Dyke waited.

Alexie didn't answer. She had her prize bracelet clasped around her wrist and was fingering it thoughtfully.

"What's eating you, Droopy-face?" Peter said, trying to cheer her up.

But Alexie remained quiet, staring out across the starlit harbor. Peter followed her gaze and caught sight of a power launch pulling away from the *Golden Goose*. The yacht's running lights swept over the passing boat, and Peter caught a glimpse of a man sprawled on the deck clutching his bandaged head—a man wearing yellow pants.

3

Charity Lady . . .

Charity Lady got d'fish in d'pot
Printed up d'ticket, selleen a lot
Got d'latest fashion from Paris Town
Alexie gonna dress up in a fancy gown

PETER hadn't seen Alexie for days—not since the week before when she had brought the Library Fund Luncheon poster to put in the shop window.

He hadn't seen Jake and Steve either. Whenever he passed the Du Bois house on his way to town, the jeep was nowhere in sight. Almost every afternoon he swam and painted at the beach where he had first met them. But they didn't return. It was as though they had forgotten he was alive.

Even Jens was busy, trying to tame a cat that had been prowling the hillside. It was a half-wild creature, and once it had found a place on the roof over their bedroom, it wouldn't budge. Jens spent most of the day waving a handful of fish heads at the starving animal.

"C'mon, Beauty. C'mon down, Beauty," Jens coaxed. "C'mon, please?"

Peter looked up and saw a scrawny gray cat with large terrified eyes and a thin pointed face. It quivered with fear and hunger as it stared at the fish heads, but it clung stubbornly to the edge of the roof.

"You call that half-dead thing Beauty?" Peter asked.

"Yup," Jens answered. " 'S'going to be a real beauty when I get it tame. 'S'going to have shiny fur and a fat tummy. I can do it. Look how Dr. Orozco takes care of Daddy. Well, I'll be Beauty's doctor. Give him milk and pills and all that other junk."

Peter reached his hand toward the frightened cat and drew it back quickly as sharp claws struck out at him.

"You don't know how to treat it," Jens said. "Hafta act real gentle an' show you won't hurt it."

"O.K. O.K., I'll get out of your way," Peter said.

He left the house and walked downhill toward town. He had reached Kronprindsens Gade and was just a block from the shop when he saw Jake and Steve.

"Hi, Pete," Jake called, waving.

Peter had figured what he would do if he saw them again. He was going to be casual and say he was sorry he had been too busy to look them up.

"Gee, hi!" Peter called out, grinning. "Where've you guys been? I've been looking all over for you."

Jake and Steve returned Peter's smile, and Jake boxed him on the shoulder. "Good to see you, Pete," Jake said. "We were on our way to your place to see if you'd have lunch with us at Bluebeard's Castle."

"What?" Peter asked, not believing his ears. The only thing going on at Bluebeard's today was the Library Fund Luncheon. And there was going to be a fashion show. He wouldn't be caught dead within a mile of that.

Jake explained that Alexie's mother was in charge of the luncheon and had been too busy to cook at home. She had told Jake and Steve to come to Bluebeard's for lunch.

"Come on," Jake said. "Let's see how the other half lives."

"Well—O.K.," Peter replied.

"Are you going to wear those?" Steve pointed to Peter's frayed, cutoff jeans. Steve was wearing a neat white shirt and slacks. Jake's shirttail hung out and his pants were wrinkled and baggy.

Peter laughed and ran up the hillside and home to change.

They rode in Jake and Steve's rented jeep. The way was steep and winding, and on the hilltop stood Bluebeard's Castle, a luxury hotel named for a round stone tower near the main building. It was said that Bluebeard the Pirate had once lived in the tower.

"Is it true about Bluebeard living here?" Steve asked.

"I really don't know," Peter replied. "I sort of doubt it. But you never can tell. My dad says lots of stories are made up for tourists. Like Drake's Seat."

"What's that?" Steve asked.

"No one has told you about Drake's Seat?"

"No."

"Well, it's supposed to be a big historical landmark. It's way over there on the other side of that mountain"—Peter pointed toward the Atlantic side of the island—"on the way to Magens Bay. Tourists are told that Sir Francis Drake 'strolled' up there to take a look at his fleet. That was a few hundred years ago."

"Go on," Steve urged.

"Anyway," Peter continued, "the Seat is about five miles straight up from the Atlantic. Mon, what a climb! Besides, from way up there the boats would look real little—like sand flies."

"I guess some people will believe anything," Jake laughed.

"There's a cement bench up there now," Peter went on. "That's Drake's Seat—get it? A few little kids have made a pretty good business out of it, too. They dress up a donkey and tie flowers on its ears. Tourists come along and pay a quarter to take their picture."

They had reached Bluebeard's Castle. Jake parked the jeep, and they hopped out and walked through the lobby to the terrace, where a lady stopped them for tickets. Steve gave her a note from Mrs. Du Bois. The lady studied it carefully, eyeing them with suspicion. "You two go ahead," she said at last. "But what about him?" She looked at Peter.

"He's my guest," Jake said, pulling out his wallet and paying the admission fee.

"You shouldn't have done that," Peter protested.

"Yes I should," Jake answered. "Remember, you stopped us from burning that manchineel, and you got us a place to stay too. The least we can do is buy your lunch."

"Well, thanks a lot," Peter mumbled.

The terrace was crowded with groups of chattering women. Peter and the two men squeezed through to the last empty table.

"We seem to be a minority of three," Jake remarked, looking around. He was right. Except for the waiters, they were the only men at the luncheon.

Steve was examining one of the flat stones that paved the terrace. "This looks like writing," he said, pointing to a stone alongside the table.

Peter grinned. "That's the gravestone of one of Bluebeard's poor, murdered wives," he commented. Jake and Steve squinted, trying to make out the worn letters. "If you guys want, I'll stick flowers on my ears and let you take my picture by it."

"Another Drake's Seat, huh, Pete?" Jake laughed.

"You never can tell," Peter replied.

He glanced across the terrace to where the Women's Club had strung up a clothesline. Pictures were hung along the line with clothespins, like wash out to dry. The breeze swung the colorful paper squares gently, and Peter strained to get a good look. There was something familiar about— They were his pictures!

Jake and Steve were looking in the same direction. Peter tried to think of a way to distract them. "Uh—did you guys get a load of the big yacht out in—" But it was too late.

"Jake," Steve said. "Let's go over and take a look at the art gallery on the clothesline."

Peter fiddled with his water glass as the two men strolled up and down the line of pictures. They halted before one of Peter's older paintings, one he had done last year. He watched them look at it. They seemed to be arguing. That painting isn't any good, Peter thought glumly. They probably think it stinks.

Jake and Steve returned to the table, and the fashion show began.

Peter paid little attention to the clothes being modeled

42

until Alexie swished through the crowd. She wore a green dress that trailed out behind like a fish's tail. He puffed out his cheeks and made fish-swimming motions with his hands as she passed by. She appeared not to notice him at all, but Peter thought her cheeks turned a little pinker than usual.

"H'm-mm, look at that," Steve said. A pert, blond girl wiggled by in a flaming red dress. It was Sondra.

"Uh-huh," Jake replied. "Some dish."

"She's my age," Peter said.

"No kidding?"

"Yeah. She's only dressed up to look old. I know her. Her name is Sondra and we went to this great party on her uncle's yacht. It's the *Golden Goose,* the boat I was—"

"Does Sondra live here?" Steve asked.

"Oh, no. She's just spending the summer on her uncle's boat. Her folks are divorced or something, and she told me they always send her off to any old relative for vacations."

"Here comes food," Jake said, and they turned their attention to eating.

They were walking to the parking lot when Alexie popped out from behind a hibiscus bush.

"Peter," she called, "I want to talk to you."

"What's up?"

"C'mon over here."

"You guys go ahead," Peter told Jake and Steve. "I'll just be a minute." He turned to Alexie. "I suppose you're mad about the face I made when you were in that fashion thing."

"Oh, that—I didn't even notice it." She ignored Peter's laugh. "What I want to know is if you're mad at me."

43

"What for?"

"You know. The pictures."

"So *you* did it!" Peter shouted.

"Don't yell, stupid. Want everyone to hear?"

"I suppose you stole them," Peter accused.

"No. I asked your mother. We needed something nice for decorations, and we thought you'd be pleased."

"Well, I'm not!"

"Oh, Peter Van Dyke," Alexie said, her voice hoarse. "I thought you'd be proud, and instead you're acting like a baby. I hope you fall right into the sea and—and drown!" She ran away from him across the lawn.

Peter watched her disappear. Jake and Steve were waiting in the jeep with the motor running.

"What was all that about?" Jake asked. The tires screeched as he drove off down the hill.

"Notheen," Peter mumbled.

"Pete," Steve said. "We, uh, we want to talk to you about something."

"One of your pictures," Jake added.

"Oh, them," Peter groaned. "If you want the truth, I could wring Alexie's neck. And Mom was in on it too. They both know I hate show-off artists. I haven't been painting very long. My stuff isn't good enough to—"

"You have a painting of a sunken ship's bell," Steve interrupted, "with lettering on it. Where did you get that idea?"

"Where I get'm all," Peter answered. "I saw it when I was swimming underwater."

"Where did you find this bell?" Jake questioned.

"What are you guys driving at?" Peter asked. "You're

44

so—so serious all of a sudden."

"Maybe we are," Steve replied, "but this is serious business. To us anyway. It's—"

"Look," Jake cut in. "This is no place to talk. Can you meet us tomorrow morning, Pete? We'll pick you up at the Pirate's Gold."

"O.K. But I have to check with my dad. I'm pretty sure he'll let me off."

"And look, Pete," Steve added, "don't mention this to anyone, huh? No one knows but us, and we want to keep it that way. For now, at least."

They stopped the jeep in front of the Pirate's Gold and Peter hopped out and went into the shop. His father was writing a sales slip. He heard his mother's voice in the back of the shop where there were dressing rooms.

"What's Mom doing?" Peter asked his father.

"Oh," Mr. Van Dyke chuckled. "She's in the fitting room trying to help a battleship squeeze into a berth meant for a tugboat."

They laughed together, sharing their private joke. The way roly-poly tourists bought clothes in sizes meant for bean-pole-skinny tourists always amused Peter and his father.

Peter walked to the full-length mirror near the dressing room. He was startled to see how excited he looked. That would never do. Anyone could tell he had a secret. Carefully, he worked his mouth into a straight line and blinked his eyes to take away some of the sparkle. Now he felt ready to ask his father for tomorrow morning off.

45

4

Pirate he snatcheen up . . .

Pirate he snatcheen up a boatful of loot
Deçapitate d'populace an' don' give a hoot
Sail away quick to Caribbean Sea
Who know what hoppen to mon like he?

MR. VAN DYKE arrived at the shop just as Peter finished opening the heavy front doors.

"I see you're early. Are your friends here yet?" he asked Peter.

"No, but they'll be along soon."

"How about helping me unpack some of these crates while you're waiting?"

"Sure, Dad," Peter replied. "You know what Dr. Orozco says. You'd better take it easy or you'll wind up in the hospital. Mom's pretty worried."

"Oh, Peter, you know how women like to fuss," Mr. Van Dyke chuckled. "I'm feeling fine."

"Morning, Grandpa Van," Peter called out as his grandfather came in the door.

"Morning, Peter," he called in reply.

Grandfather Van Dyke spent most of his days in the

shop, although he had long since turned its management over to his son. He enjoyed talking to the tourists, and on quiet days island friends often dropped by.

Everyone called him Grandpa Van, for he was a beloved figure on St. Thomas. He had once told Peter that he was an institution on the island. When Peter asked him what an institution was, Grandpa Van had chuckled and explained that it was something people put up with because it had been around so long.

Peter set to work unwrapping crates of Swedish glass. Suddenly, he felt a sharp jab between his shoulder blades and spun around. The jab had come from the long red fingernail of a short round woman in a sequined muumuu. Peter had been taught how to deal with such customers. Politely he said, "May I help you?"

"Yes you can, boy," she shrilled, jutting her chin out. This was quite an accomplishment, because she had chins all the way down to her seashell necklace.

Peter looked at the woman and wondered if, somewhere in the States, there was a factory that manufactured tourists like her. In every group of visitors to the islands, there seemed to be several who ran to excess fat, gaudy colors, silly hats, and bad manners.

"What would you like?" Peter asked.

"Information, if you don't mind. And quickly. My time is valuable." She picked up an advertising leaflet from the counter, glanced at it, frowned, slapped it down again. "Yesterday I went to an affair at that pirate's hotel—"

"You mean the luncheon at Bluebeard's?" Peter suggested.

"Yes. Dreadful fashion show with silly, gawky models."

Peter nodded politely, biting his lip.

"I noticed some paintings. Watercolors. But nobody there knew a thing. All they told me was to come here."

Peter felt a shiver run up his spine. What should he do? What could he do? Grandpa Van and his father were watching. He would just have to face up to it.

He took a deep breath, "The pictures are mine."

"Oh. Well, who painted them?" she asked.

"I did," Peter answered.

"Now listen to me, boy. Don't think because I'm a tourist you can pull that old stuff on me!"

"But I did paint them," Peter insisted.

"Look here," the woman went on, her voice rising, "I know the work of an experienced—"

Grandpa Van could hold back no longer. "My grandson painted them, Madam," he said firmly. "I've watched him work. Peter has even been compared to Van Gogh."

"Well! He's hardly that good. But if you insist, I'll take your word for it. I've come to make a business proposition. I own a high-class gift and curio shop in New York. Only the finest things in the novelty line." She rummaged in her purse, pulled out a tissue-wrapped shape, and handed it to Peter.

"Open it," she said. "No obligation. Just want to show you the kind of merchandise I carry."

Peter unwrapped the object and examined it, mystified. The woman snatched it from him.

"Oh, really!" she snorted. "It's a toothpick holder. See? You put the picks in here and they poke out here. When you take one, it makes a noise—like this." It gave off a rude sound.

Peter looked at the floor, embarrassed, while the woman cackled with delight over her joke.

"Pretty cute, eh?" she said. "Well now, let's get back to our discussion. There was a picture of yours at the luncheon. One with yellowish-green fish in it. They had long tails, and faces like this." The woman twisted her face to demonstrate.

Peter almost exploded with held-back laughter. Funny thing was, she really did look like a fish.

"Do you know the one I mean?"

"I think so," Peter replied.

"I want you to paint fifty just like it."

"What?" he gasped.

"Well, not exactly like it. I want some purple—no, make that fuchsia-color. And silver too. And get some of that paint that glows in the dark. People go for that. When can you have them ready?"

Peter was at a loss. "I'm sorry, but I couldn't do them—ever."

"Listen, boy. Don't get fresh. Can't you see a good deal when it's stuck in front of you? I'll pay you a nice fat commission on every one I sell. You could make maybe five dollars a picture. How about that?"

"No, thanks," Peter said.

"Don't you realize what I'm offering you? Do you know where New York is?"

"Yes," Peter answered. "My mother went to college there. Barnard."

"Now you listen to me—" The woman's shrill voice rose to a shout.

Peter's father walked to where his son and the woman

49

stood. He took the woman's arm and smoothly escorted her to the door. He spoke very gently, and she followed meekly, quite taken by surprise. She hardly seemed to notice that she was being led from the shop until she stood outside on the sidewalk. She remained there a moment, her face flushed the color of baked ham. Frustrated, she whirled around and flounced up the street.

"Bravo!" two voices cheered.

It was Jake and Steve. They had entered the shop during the "art discussion" and stood by Grandpa Van, watching.

"Deliver us from tourists like that," Grandpa Van chanted, spreading his arms wide.

"Oh, Dad, Grandpa Van, these are my friends, Jake and Steve."

Peter watched the men shake hands. "I'm ready to go if you are," he said.

"O.K., Pete," said Jake. "Let's go."

Peter promised to return to the shop later and finish unpacking the crates. He waved good-by and got into the jeep with Jake and Steve.

"Where are we going?" he asked.

"Up toward Crown Mountain. We'll drive until we find a lonely place to park." Jake answered as he steered the jeep away from the shop.

"How do you like living on St. Thomas?" Steve asked.

"Fine," Peter replied. "But I've never lived anywhere else. We went to St. Martin a couple of years ago. I have some French cousins over there. And I've been to Puerto Rico and St. Croix—and, of course, St. John and Tortola lots of times. We went to Jamaica once too."

"You know the West Indies pretty well," Steve remarked.

"I guess so."

"Does anyone know just how many Virgin Islands there are?" Steve asked.

"Well," Peter said. "Of course there are the three American ones: St. Thomas, St. Croix, and St. John. But when Columbus first saw the islands, he figured maybe there were thousands. So he named them the Virgin Islands, after the legend of St. Ursula."

"Saint who?" Steve asked.

"Ursula. A long time ago she was supposed to have gotten together ten or eleven thousand virgins—a whole lot, anyway—and sailed around the seas in a fleet of ships."

"Why?" asked Jake as he managed a sharp turn.

"Oh, there was this king who wanted to marry her. Only she didn't want to marry him, see? So she got him to promise to let her sail around for a while first. But it didn't turn out so well."

"What happened?" Steve asked.

"There was this storm and they got off course. They sailed up the Rhine River to some German city. I can't remember the name. Cologne, I think. Anyhow, their timing was pretty bad 'cause just about then Attila and the Huns came to town and killed off St. Ursula and the whole bunch."

"Some story," Steve commented. "How did you find out about that?"

"Oh, from school. And my folks too. They have a whole lot of books. They're always reading. I like to read too.

51

Mostly in the hurricane season when I can't go to the beach."

"When do the hurricanes come?" Jake sounded worried.

"Usually a couple of weeks from now. After Supplication Day."

"What day?"

"Supplication. That's July 25. It's a holiday. We all go to church and pray for no hurricanes. Sometimes it works. Other times, mon, it really gets rough. A few years ago we had a bad one. The eye of the storm was headed straight for St. Thomas. The weather reports said it was going to hit us dead on at about three in the morning. A lot of people went to the Fort for shelter, but at the last minute the storm changed its course. Killed a lot of guys over on St. Martin though."

"Here's a good place," Jake said, stopping the jeep. They got out and sat on the ground in the shade of a giant mango tree. Steve opened the briefcase he had been carrying and pulled out a sheaf of papers. Carefully, he arranged them in their right order.

"Take a look at these," he said, handing them to Peter.

Peter looked at the papers. The writing was in a strange style. It was not English. "Only thing I can read is this number—one, six, six, eight," he said.

"That's a date, 1668," Steve explained. "These are pho-tostats of old documents written in Spanish."

"We have Spanish in school, but I can't read any of this."

"It's written in old Spanish script. Hard to make out unless you've studied it."

"Is this your research project?" Peter asked.

52

"Part of it," Jake replied, smiling. "And you're the other part."

"Me?"

"Let me explain," Jake went on. "It would take all day to read these things, so I'll give it to you quickly."

"This letter"—he held up one of the papers—"was written by a Franciscan monk in Florida, in 1668, shortly after pirates raided his settlement. The letter was never sent, because soon after he wrote it, the monk died of injuries inflicted by the pirates."

"What does it say?" Peter asked. A soft breeze ruffled the leaves of the big tree shading them. Steve put a rock on the stack of papers to hold them down.

"The letter tells about the pirate raid and the killing and looting done by El Sangre. He was one of the most bloodthirsty pirate captains working the shipping routes in those days."

"I know what El Sangre means," Peter said. "The Bloody One."

"Yes, and an apt name it was. He would kill for the fun of it. He kept his crew under control by torturing or killing any who dared speak up against him."

"Get back to the letter," said Steve.

"Oh, yes. The monk who wrote the letter was a missionary to Florida, sent by the Spanish king. They called him Father Fernando. Judging from his letter it was the shock of the looting of his church that killed him as much as infection from his wounds. You see, the pirates took his image of St. Francis, his gold crucifix and silver chalice, and all the money he had saved."

"How did you find out about that letter?" Peter asked.

"It was part of a historical collection at the university. But until we got hold of the diary, it was just another old document of bloodshed and tragedy."

"Diary?"

"Yes. We found a diary in the library of a man in Puerto Rico, just before we came here. It throws new light on Father Fernando's letter."

Peter listened, his excitement growing more intense with every word.

"The diary belonged to a Spaniard who lived in the West Indies in the seventeenth century, a man who treated wounds and knew a little about medicine. He kept a careful record of all his patients, telling what treatment he gave them.

"Imagine the scene, Peter. It is September of 1668. The doctor is taking his afternoon siesta. Suddenly, he is awakened by loud voices and knocking. He opens the door and finds several village fishermen holding a ragged, half-drowned bundle of a man, a shipwrecked sailor they had hauled out of the sea. The villagers tell the doctor how desperately the man had clutched the piece of broken ship's mast that had kept him afloat.

" 'Bring him inside, quickly,' the doctor orders. He wets the man's cracked, parched lips with water and pulls off the filthy rags that still cling to his battered body.

"The doctor rubs soothing ointment on the man's wounds and binds them. This done, he takes up his diary and asks the stranger, 'Who are you? What is your name?'

"The stranger is almost too weak to speak. His swollen lips move noiselessly as he strains to form words. His eyes are wide with the terror of a madman.

"At last the man speaks, the words coming out in painful croaks. 'Cap'n's dead. All dead. All hands dead. An' iss Sain' Francis did it. I tole'm not take it. I tole'm leave Sain' Francis where 'e be'long . . . in 'is altar. Leave'm. I tole'm.' His voice trails off to a harsh whisper.

" 'Who are you?' the doctor asks. 'Were there any other survivors?'

" 'All gone . . . gone. Down'n bottom . . . off Skel'ton Head.'

" 'Where?' the doctor presses.

" 'Skel'ton Head . . . iss isl . . . island.'

" 'But where is it?'

" 'I'm jussa . . . jussa miserable . . . hadda good time in Santa Cruz. Nex' mornin' sail off'n go . . . down . . . Iss Sain' Francis blowin' us on a reef . . . Issa curse . . . storm . . . big . . . 'e only wood but 'e got us.'

" 'You must rest now,' the doctor says, but the sick man ignores him and raves on. His breathing becomes labored and he gasps for breath. 'Mother of God . . . f'give . . . Sain' Francis . . . f'give . . . mercy . . .'

"The strange sailor died without naming himself, his ship, or his captain. 'Forever an unsolved mystery,' the doctor wrote in his diary as he closed the entry."

Peter let go of the breath he had been holding. "What a story!"

"Jake hasn't explained the connection between the letter and the diary," Steve said. "You see, Father Fernando's letter alone told us little. But, when you put it with the diary—"

"I know, I know!" Peter interrupted. "The St. Francis image."

"Seems logical," Steve said. "A sunken ship with a wooden St. Francis aboard, added to a dying priest mourning the loss of his image of St. Francis. One and one makes—"

"Two!" Peter laughed.

"We can add up the facts," Jake said, "but we can't find that sunken ship. We know El Sangre's ship went down about one half day's journey from Santa Cruz—which we call St. Croix—near an island the shipwrecked sailor called Skeleton Head. We've asked around, but no one has heard of such an island."

"What did you mean when you said I was the other part of this?" Peter asked.

"I'm coming to that. Yesterday, at the luncheon, you gave us a very important piece of evidence." Jake walked to the jeep and returned with one of Peter's seascapes.

"Where'd you get that?"

"We told Alexie we wanted to borrow it. We promised to give it to you."

"Oh."

"Where did you paint this?"

"That? Oh, off there someplace." Peter gestured toward the Caribbean side of the island.

Steve leaned over the painting, tracing the outline of a gray-green shape. "Is this what we think it is—a bell?"

"Yes," Peter said.

"And why did you put these letters on the bell?"

"I don't know. I mean—they were on there when I saw the bell, and I just copied them."

Steve read, "N-A, a space, then four more letters, O-S-A-B. You didn't make these up?"

"No," Peter answered. "I saw this old bell with those letters on it and figured it was from a sunken ship—there are a lot of them around here, but I couldn't read it all. Some of the letters were covered with coral."

"Take a look at this." Jake handed Peter a photostat of Father Fernando's letter, pointing to a sentence halfway down the page. Peter puzzled out the elaborate script until he had a name—a woman's name.

"Ana Rosabella?" he asked. "Who was she?"

"Not who—what," Jake said. "The *Ana Rosabella* was El Sangre's ship."

Steve read the letters from Peter's seascape once more.

"N-A, space, O-S-A-B. All we lack is an 'A' at the beginning and an 'R' in the middle and—"

Peter almost shouted, "An E-L-L-A at the end!" He slapped the trunk of the mango tree in excitement.

Jake boxed him on the shoulder. "What do you think, Pete?"

"I think I was swimming near the wreck of El Sangre's ship last year."

"We think so too. But the trick is to find it. And that's where you come in."

"Yes," Steve added, leaning forward and lowering his voice almost to a whisper. "Can you lead us to Skeleton Head island?"

"I don't know," Peter said. "I'll bet I've been swimming at a thousand places around here. It's hard to remember just one of them. And I've never heard of an island called Skeleton Head."

"You might think of it later," Jake said.

"I sure hope so," Peter replied. "I'll try."

"And, Pete," Steve said, "keep all this under your hat. No one knows about the wreck of the *Ana Rosabella* except the three of us."

"Secret?"

"Yes," Jake added. "If anyone finds out what we're on to, half the population will be looking for that ship and its cargo."

"The gold," Peter said.

"Yes," Jake replied. "But more important to us than a few gold coins is absolute proof of El Sangre's fate. We've worked on this project all year, and if we fail now, the whole thing will sink faster than the *Ana Rosabella*."

"I know I'll remember," Peter said. "I mean, I just have to."

"Take your time," Steve said. "But not too much time. From what you told us about the hurricane season, we'd better find that ship soon."

"You're right," Peter agreed. "A big storm could completely wipe out anything that's left."

They drove Peter back to the shop. As he hopped out of the jeep, he glanced at the name painted over the doorway: PIRATE'S GOLD. Now he knew why Jake had laughed so hard that day at Coki Bay.

Peter set to work unpacking crates of Swedish crystal. He dusted the fragile pieces and tried to recall the afternoon a year ago when he had seen the bell. Rubbing a crystal paperweight, he looked into its clear depths. "Where is Skeleton Head?" he whispered, his breath clouding the glass. But it was no use. Even a crystal ball wouldn't tell him.

5

Gotta find sometheen . . .

Gotta find sometheen, don' know where it be
Hideen in d'water of Caribbean Sea
Deep dark secret is Skeleton Head
An d'mon dat know, he long gone dead

"C'MON, BEAUTY, c'mon down, Beauty. I won't hurt you."

Peter rolled over in bed and pulled the pillow over his ears. "Can't you be quiet out there?" he yelled at Jens.

He had tossed half the night, mocked by a phantom voice that whispered, "Skeleton Head, Skeleton Head," over and over. He had even heard a bell, he was sure of it. It rang with a strange, desperate sound that seemed to come bubbling and gurgling out of the deep.

Where had he seen that bell? All he knew for certain was that it lay near a cluster of brain coral. That much was in his painting. He knew no more now than when Jake and Steve first asked him.

"C'mon, Beauty, nice Beauty," Jens coaxed.

Peter grabbed his pillow and threw it across the room. No use trying to sleep with Jens talking to that fool cat!

He sat on the edge of the bed and rubbed his eyes, groggy from lack of sleep.

He pulled his watercolor of the bell from under the bed and studied it. Pretty awful. Why had he made the water so dark? Why else? Water was always dark far below the surface. Now he remembered how he had pulled and tugged at the bell, trying to get it loose. He had shot up for air, and his lungs had almost burst before he made it. He had planned to return for the bell with an aqualung, but a hurricane had swept over the islands before he had had a chance. He had forgotten all about it until Jake and Steve came along.

He still didn't have the answer. Where was Skeleton Head?

He could actually see the gaping eye sockets and white jawbone of a skeleton—a skeleton suit and mask pinned to the wall over the dresser. Of course, he was staring at the costume he had worn during Carnival last April.

It hit him like lightning.

Little Skull!

Why hadn't he thought of it before? Little Skull island was named for its skull-like shape. It was easy to see how a shipwrecked sailor would call it Skeleton Head.

Peter jumped into his clothes and took off at a run for the Du Bois house.

"I'll go right now and arrange for a boat," Jake said, after hearing Peter's story.

"Maybe my Uncle Pierre will let us use his," Peter suggested. "He's my godfather."

"It's worth a try," Steve replied.

They climbed into the jeep and drove along the waterfront to Frenchtown.

Peter's godfather was sitting in his yard mending a fishnet. He agreed to let them use his boat, the weather-beaten *Cha-Cha-Chug*.

"Looks like someone is already there," Steve remarked, as they came within sight of Little Skull island.

"Where?"

"Take a look through the glasses."

Peter raised them to his eyes and followed Little Skull's shoreline until he caught sight of a man splashing through knee-deep water toward a waiting motor launch.

"What's going on?" Jake asked.

Peter passed the glasses to Jake.

"H'm-m-m," Jake said, "he's sure in a hurry. And he's wearing some kind of turban."

"It looked like a bandage to me," Steve said.

Peter said nothing. What was the man's rush? And why was his head bandaged? He remembered something and looked through the glasses again. Yes, he could see quite clearly that the man was wearing yellow pants.

Peter had no time to puzzle over what he had seen. They anchored the boat, waded ashore, and unwrapped the lunch Mrs. Du Bois had sent along.

"Hey, that Mrs. Du Bois can really cook," Jake said, sitting cross-legged on the sand eating fried chicken.

Peter had left home without breakfast, so he ate eagerly. And while he ate he found himself thinking about Alexie. He hadn't seen her for days. Not since the luncheon at Bluebeard's. Merkley told him he had seen her paddle-

boating with Sondra Fetching at Magens Bay.

After they had eaten, Peter led Jake and Steve up the beach. He waded slowly into the shallow water, looking for any sign that would guide them to the submerged bell.

The beach was small and crescent-shaped, with a cluster of grape trees at one end. On the other end were rock and coral formations. At high tide, water flowed underneath the rocks into small caves.

"I'll see what I can find out here," Peter said, putting on his fins and mask. He swam into deeper and deeper water, searching the bottom—rocks, coral pinnacles, seaweed. Back and forth he swam, trying to find the cluster of coral near which the old ship's bell lay. Finally, tired and discouraged, he gave up.

Steve and Jake watched him return slowly to the beach.

"No luck, huh, Pete?" Steve said, shaking his head. "Guess we're on the wrong track."

"Don't give up so easily," Jake chided. "C'mon, we'll try again tomorrow."

"Well—O.K.," Steve reluctantly agreed.

Peter's spirits were low as they headed the *Cha-Cha-Chug* back to St. Thomas. A lot of help he had been.

Peter trudged up the forty-nine steps to his front door. He entered and stopped just inside. The house seemed strangely quiet. Where was everyone? Shop closing time was more than an hour ago. His parents never went away without telling him. He looked on the dining room table for a note.

A distressing sound sent him running up the stairs two at a time. It was Jens.

"What's the matter, Jens?" Peter asked.

"It's Daddy," Jens said between sobs. "Daddy's—"

"Tell me!" Peter cried out, his voice shaking.

Jens sat up, rubbed his fists in his eyes and blew his nose.

"I was at the shop today," Jens began.

"Yes?"

"Well—Daddy was talking to Grandpa Van about some new stuff gonna come in when he got all funny and sat down."

"Go on."

"Mommy was there, and she went over to Daddy and asked was there anything wrong, and Daddy said no he was O.K. and not to worry. Then he—he—"

"He what?"

"I don't know what you call it. His eyes went like this, and he got all loose and fell down."

"Oh, no," Peter breathed.

"Mommy called the amb—amblunts, and they put Daddy in a bed with wheels and took him to the hospital. Mommy rode along. She was hanging on to his hand."

Jens flopped down on his bed and sobbed uncontrollably.

Peter took his brother by the shoulders. "Jens, stop crying. You've got to be grown-up. That's what Dad would want."

"I s'pose so," Jens quavered. "I'll be grown-up."

Peter did not dare let Jens see how scared he was.

"I'm going to the hospital and see what I can find out."

"Don't leave me here alone," Jens pleaded.

"You can come with me if you promise not to cry."

"I promise," Jens said. He stood up and stuffed his shirt in his pants to show he was ready for anything.

6

Peter daddy flat . . .

Peter daddy flat in hospital bed
Doctor say, 'Mon, you almos' got dead'
So Peter stick to business on d'holiday
Gotta work at shop, no time for play

IT WAS GO-DOWN DAY, a special island holiday that meant "Go-Down-To-The-Sea-And-Have-Fun!"

St. Thomas had caught the mood. Shops were closed, and all St. Thomians who were not having their own picnics were on their way to the barbecue at Magens Bay.

All St. Thomians, that is, except Peter. He was at the Pirate's Gold, working. There were boxes and crates of imported merchandise—china, perfume, and woolens—to be unpacked and put on display for the mob of tourists that would descend on the town when the *Caribbean Queen* docked the next morning. Peter's father was still in the hospital. It was up to Peter to help out now.

He had insisted that his mother, Grandpa Van, and Jens go out to Magens Bay. He could work faster alone, he told them. But he felt a pang of envy as they drove away. He thought about the fun they would have water-skiing,

66

paddle-boating, and donkey racing. There would be a steel band too, and gallons of lemonade, and barbecued pig.

"Got no complaints—" Peter sang to cheer himself. And he really hadn't. His father was recovering, and the doctors said he would be his old self again after a short rest.

There was only one thing Peter regretted—telling Jake and Steve he couldn't go with them to Little Skull. Not for a while anyway.

"Can't be helped," Jake had said, smiling.

"We'll try to do the best we can on our own," Steve had added.

Jake had boxed him on the shoulder and told him to hold the fort. Mon, what terrific guys!

Peter heard footsteps in the doorway.

It was Alexie and Sondra. They entered the shop and swaggered around like big-spending tourists, pretending not to see Peter. Alexie held up a tiny red bikini and said through her nose, "It's much too large."

Sondra giggled. "And expensive. We can get it cheaper at Macy's." She was the first to break the act. "You're really not coming out to Magens Bay, Peter?"

"Can't."

"My folks even closed the drugstore today," Alexie added. "Nobody else on the whole island is working, stupid."

Peter looked at Sondra. She was the same girl he had seen on Vhartok's yacht—but she wasn't. For one thing, her hair was different. It was long and smooth now, like Alexie's.

"You have to come," Alexie urged. "Everyone's going to be there."

"I'm sorry. I can't," Peter said and began checking off a long packing list.

"Oh, all right," Sondra sighed. "If you can't, you can't. But it'll be ghastly with no cute boys there, won't it Alexie?"

"Oh, Sondra—" Alexie stammered.

Peter felt his ears burning. He walked to a stack of crates and set to work. Out of the corner of his eye, he watched the girls. They stood in the doorway whispering, and after a while they left.

It was quieter than before.

Peter uncrated, dusted, and priced all the china and then stacked the bolts of woolens. He was so engrossed in his work he did not notice the two women in the doorway until one of them coughed. He looked up and automatically smiled. They smiled back. One was tall and square and the other was short and round.

"Are you open?" the short one asked in a babyish voice.

"No," Peter replied. "We're closed today."

"But we're from the *Caribbean Queen*," the tall one boomed. "Our cruise director told us that St. Thomas is the best port for shopping."

"And now everything is closed," Baby-Voice whined.

"It's a holiday," Peter explained.

"What holiday?" asked the tall one, her eyes narrowing.

"Go-Down Day," he replied.

"What day?"

"It's uh—" Peter stalled for time, trying to think of a way to discourage them. "Anyway, we weren't expecting your ship until tomorrow."

"But couldn't we look around a weeny-teeny bit?" Baby-Voice begged.

"It's our only chance," her companion stated flatly. "We have a busy program. This is our scheduled shopping period in St. Thomas."

"Well—O.K.," Peter said.

The tall woman marched to the doorway, stuck her head out, and bellowed, "It's all right, everybody. Come on!"

Peter was almost knocked down by the stampede. Cruise-ship passengers crowded into the shop, eager to spend their traveler's checks. He sold most of the china he had just un-packed and took orders for eleven dresses to be made and delivered to the ship along with cartons of china and silver.

At last they left, and Peter sank down in Grandpa Van's favorite chair. Now that he had time to think, he was worried. How was he going to get all those orders filled and delivered by sailing time?

"Hee-haw. Hee-haw."

Peter started at the sudden noise. A donkey? In here? He laughed as the "donkey" jumped from behind the door. It was Merkley Peach.

"Where d'freebs? Where d'freebs?" Merkley croaked.

"No freebs, Merk."

Merkley went to the back room and peered into the ice-box where the lemonade was kept. The pitcher was empty.

"Ain' no freebs 'roun here," he complained.

"Sorry, no freebs today," Peter said. "Hey, mon, you should have seen the mob that just left! Didn't need any-thing free to get them to buy. Listen, Merk, I need help. Could you go out to Magens Bay and ask my mother to come back here? Tell her it's a business emergency."

"Sure, mon. I goeen der now." And Merkley loped up the street.

"Thanks, Merk," Peter shouted after him.

Peter locked the shop and set off in the opposite direction. He had to find the seamstresses who worked at the Pirate's Gold. Eleven made-to-order dresses were promised for delivery by sailing time!

He had no luck at the first two houses. Everyone was away for the holiday. At last he found one of the regular girls at home, and she agreed to come to the shop and work on the dresses.

Mrs. Van Dyke, Alexie, and Sondra were at the shop when Peter returned.

They all pitched in.

The seamstress, Mrs. Van Dyke, and Alexie worked on the dresses. Sondra lined dress boxes with tissue paper and studied Peter's scribbled sales slips to get the right name and cabin number for each box. Peter packed the china and silver.

Just fifteen minutes before sailing time, they had everything loaded in the Van Dyke station wagon. Peter rode with his mother to help balance the piles of boxes.

They delivered the packages to the *Caribbean Queen* only five minutes before the gangplank was raised. Peter let out a deep breath. What a day!

He told his mother he would walk home. After the wild pace of the afternoon he needed to unwind. He walked slowly past the West Indian Company to the Fort and on to Hibiscus Alley. He often went home this way. The sun was low in the sky, and the lane was almost dark.

Out of the shadows, a figure emerged and beckoned.

"C'mere," a voice growled. "Wanna talk t'yuh."

The figure drew nearer. When Peter saw who it was, he drew back.

"Come on, kid. I ain't gonna hurt yuh." It was Nick Vhartok.

"What do you want to talk to me about?"

"What you doin' over to Little Skull, huh?"

"How did you find out about that?" Peter blurted.

"Never mind. I gotta system. You didn't answer me. What's up?"

"Nothing."

"Come on, let's be friends, huh? I got fifty bucks says you leave that part of the Caribbean alone."

"No deal," Peter said. "It's public property."

"Not according to me," Vhartok barked. "Now you listen, and you listen good. I don't know what you and your friends are up to over there but I'm warnin' yuh, nobody pushes Nick Vhartok around. Stay out of my way!"

Peter said nothing. He clenched his fists and struggled to keep his anger from showing. He was as tall as Vhartok, but the man outweighed him by fifty pounds.

"So that's the way yuh wanna play. Well, I can play pretty rough too. You better pay attention to me, you little half-breed punk. Island White. That's a laugh!"

Peter felt as though he had been punched in the stomach.

"Did you hear me? I said you're trash. Half-breed trash! Not white. Not black. Not nothin'. You're a nothin'!"

Peter turned and walked away, Vhartok's words ringing in his ears. He looked back to make sure he wasn't being followed and saw Nick Vhartok raise his arm and shake his fist.

7

Mon wid big head . . .

Mon wid big head have brain like gnat
Say no to he, he call you rat
So Peter don' mind he low-down words
'Cause mon who talkeen is for the birds

"GO ON, NOW," Grandpa Van said. "Off with you.
You've earned a little time for yourself."

"Are you sure you can get along without me?" Peter asked.

"Your mother and I can handle everything. So stop worrying."

"Grandpa Van—" Peter began.

"Yes?"

"Could I talk to you about something?"

"You can always talk to me, Peter."

"I mean—alone?"

Grandpa Van looked at Peter and rubbed his chin. "Come on back to the office. We'll be alone there."

When they had settled themselves in the big oak captain's chairs, Peter opened his mouth. Nothing came out. He didn't know how to begin.

"Is something bothering you?" Grandpa Van asked.

"Uh-huh," Peter mumbled, his head down.

"Well, out with it. I'm no mind reader."

"Grandpa Van," Peter started, his voice low, "should I be mad if someone calls me a—a half-breed?"

"Who said it?"

"Nick Vhartok."

"I suppose any name that one called you would be an insult. But remember, Peter, you are a mixture of races, or half-breed, as some people say. You're Danish, Dutch, Negro, and Scotch." He chuckled softly. "And as if all that weren't enough, you have a French godfather."

Grandpa Van grew serious again. "I wish your grandmother were alive. She'd know what to say to you." He paused, his eyes misting. "Your Grandma Van was the most beautiful woman I ever saw. I used to call her my black swan. She never let on, but I think she liked it. Yes, she had a way about her—wasn't anyone like my Emily."

"What do you mean, Grandpa?"

"I wish you could have seen her during one of the worst hurricanes ever to hit St. Thomas—more than fifty years ago. Your Grandma Van, Emily Christensen she was then, was a volunteer nurse. She worked day and night at the hospital taking care of people injured in the storm. We were all scared, and she must have been scared too, but she never showed it. I swear, it kept some of us alive just to be near her. She had enough courage for everybody. I know. I was one of her patients.

"I guess I never told you before how we met. We were married forty-eight years when she died, Peter, and I miss her every day."

74

"I miss Grandma Van too," Peter said.

"I know you do. So remember this. If anyone calls you a half-breed again, that 'half' they're talking about is your Grandma Van." He was silent for a moment. "I hope I've answered your question."

"Yes, Grandpa, you have. Thanks. Thanks a lot."

"I want you to remember something else, Peter. People like Nick Vhartok have to stoop very low to insult someone. He couldn't find anything really bad about you, so he picked on your color. He might just as well have picked on the way you part your hair, or the shape of your ears. He didn't insult you, Peter, he insulted himself, by showing how low he could go."

"I never thought of it that way," Peter said.

Grandpa Van looked at Peter and smiled. "Now get going! And have a good day."

Peter left the shop and walked to Frenchtown. Uncle Pierre had agreed to let him use the *Cha-Cha-Chug*. He stowed his gear in the boat, tinkered with the motor to get it started, and headed for Little Skull island. Steve and Jake would be away until late Saturday. They had gone to consult the Park Rangers over on St. John. He would have a chance to look around on his own.

No one was in sight when Peter reached Little Skull. He anchored the boat in a small, sheltered cove, where it was partly hidden by jagged rocks. Breaking off grape-tree branches, he camouflaged the part of the boat still showing. No sense taking chances, especially after Nick Vhartok's warning.

By midafternoon he had worked his way to the coral formation at the far end of the beach. It was dangerous go-

75

ing, and he almost lost his footing several times. Even though he was careful, he slipped on a wet rock and pitched into the shallow water at the entrance of a small sea cave. He narrowly missed landing smack in the middle of a nest of sea urchins. He whistled as he looked at the mass of spiky, black creatures.

As he sat facing the entrance to the cave, it appeared larger than at first. He waded in.

After the bright sunlight, he was blinded for a moment. But as his eyes adjusted to the dimness, he saw something that surprised him. There was a narrow ledge running along one side of the cave, and on the ledge was a row of bamboo crates. What were they doing here? Peter wondered. There were no tags or labels on the crates to show who owned them.

With the point of his fishing knife, he loosened some of the bamboo sticks on one of the crates and slipped his hand inside. He could feel four square packages, each wrapped in a smooth, stiff material. He guessed it was oil silk—at least it felt like it. But he couldn't be sure. If only—

A blast like thunder echoed on the rocks, announcing the approach of a powerful motor launch. Remembering Vhartok's warning, Peter scrambled to a hiding place.

He had barely squeezed into a rocky crevice when loud voices told him that two men were entering the cave.

He could see nothing from where he was hidden, but he could hear the two men, no longer talking now, as they waded in and out. Their movements sent little waves rippling through the shallow water and splashing against his ankles.

At last it was quiet.

76

Peter inched away from the wall and looked at the ledge. It was empty—the crates were gone.

He looked toward the entrance of the cave. In the bright sunlight outside, two men were wading away. One wore yellow pants.

The launch started with a roar and sped away. Peter stayed in the cave until he felt it was safe. When he waded out, the launch was a dot on the horizon heading in the direction of St. Thomas.

There was no time now to puzzle over what the man in the yellow pants—Vhartok's man—was up to. Peter had lost time hiding in the cave. He hurried into the water to continue his search for the old bell.

He didn't remember swimming from this end of the beach, but as long as he was here he would take a look.

Swimming straight out from shore, he dove below.

It was deeper than he expected. He searched the bottom, working into still deeper water. It was slow going, and he had to surface often. If only he had thought to borrow an aqualung.

Over there. What was that?

He swam closer. Yes, there it was—the large cluster of brain coral he had discovered last year. But where was the bell? If he remembered right, it was only a few feet away.

He went up for air and back down again to search. But his luck had run out. The bell was nowhere in sight.

A school of copper-colored fish shot through the water over his head. A hermit crab picked up its shell-home and moved out of Peter's way.

He was ready to give up, but in a last, desperate gesture,

he pushed aside a dark mass of seaweed. His hand struck something.

Was this it? He dug away sand and shells until he could make out the letters N and A. He had found the bell at last!

Peter swam back to the *Cha-Cha-Chug* and climbed aboard. He sketched a rough map on his watercolor pad, showing where the bell lay. The wreck must be out farther, buried under course sand and overgrown with seaweed and coral. The hurricanes had done their work. No wonder he had trouble finding the bell—the storm last year had almost completely changed the bottom of the sea.

The map finished, Peter paused to think about all that had happened to him that day. His excitement over locating the bell had overshadowed what he had seen in the cave. Now he knew why Vhartok had warned him to stay away from Little Skull. He was using the cave for something he wanted to keep secret.

Peter guessed he would never know what Vhartok was doing with those bamboo crates—or what was in them, either. There was only one way to clear up the mystery— get on Vhartok's yacht and have another look at the room where the crates were kept. But after calling him names and threatening him, Vhartok didn't seem likely to invite Peter aboard the *Golden Goose*—ever.

Well, Nick Vhartok wasn't going to stop him from leading Jake and Steve to the wreck of the *Ana Rosabella*.

8

Warneen to Peter . . .

Warneen to Peter, better comprehend
Fooleen with Vhartok will hurry up your end
He mean tough mon, don' mind d'law
So watch out f'scratches from d'Vhartok claw

ALEXIE was waiting by the front steps when Peter got home from Little Skull.

"Guess what?" she said.

"What are you up to now?" Peter asked suspiciously.

"Me? I'm not up to anything. It's Vhartok. There's going to be a party next Saturday on the *Golden Goose*."

"Another party? How come a sourpuss like Vhartok gives so many parties?"

"How come not? He can afford to. Besides, this one's special. It's Sondra-birthday party."

"I don't see why you're telling me. I'm not invited—am I?"

"Sure you are. Sondra said so. But you have to come in costume. It's a Carnival party."

Only that afternoon Peter had figured that his chances of getting on Vhartok's yacht were slim. But now . . . "O.K., then. I'll be Moko Jumbie." There was a costume at the Pirate's Gold he could use.

"I'll be Danish again. All I have is that costume I wore for the 'Salute to Denmark' float at Carnival.

"Say," she added, "where were you all day? Oh, don't look so smug. I suppose you were working on that super-secret project with Jake and Steve."

"Well, sort of. But I was alone this time. We're going out together soon."

"What are you guys up to, anyway?" she asked.

"Mon, women sure are snoopy, and you're no exception."

"O.K., stupid. But I'll find out one of these days. Just you wait."

She turned and started down the steps. "See you Saturday?" she called over her shoulder.

"Sure."

Peter sat on the doorstep and looked down at the harbor, puzzled. Why would Vhartok give another party—or any party—when he had so much to hide? Could it be that the parties were some kind of cover-up?

It was a strange-looking group that rode the launch to Vhartok's yacht the night of the party. Everyone was costumed and masked, even the stewards. There were six Zulus in lion skins, a Bluebeard, a Long John Silver, an Uncle Sam, and many more. Alexie wore her blue-and-white Danish costume, and Peter was Moko Jumbie, the "Spirit of Carnival." A short fellow standing near Peter was dressed in a skeleton suit. Peter was aware that his every move was being watched from the eyeholes of the skeleton mask. Vhartok was taking no chances.

Peter and his friends were surprised to find that the party was not just for them. The ship's lounge was jammed with laughing, dancing people, all in costume. Two steel bands played their loudest.

Uncertain, the newcomers clustered by the door until Sondra came out of the crowd. She wore a simple cotton shift and a tall straw Cha-Cha hat made by Peter's Uncle Pierre.

"What's all this, Sondra?" Alexie asked.

Sondra shrugged and made a face. "Well, it was supposed to be my birthday party. But I guess Uncle Nicky figured having just us kids again would be a bore. He invited a whole bunch of tourists over from one of the cruise ships. I don't know any of them!"

A tall, skinny woman dressed as Little Red Riding Hood swooped down upon them. Her face was hidden behind a rosy pink mask and her head was covered by a wig of long blond curls. "A wolf's after me!" she shrieked and disappeared into the mob on the dance floor.

"I—I'm sorry," Sondra apologized. Her lower lip trembled.

"When do we eat?" someone shrilled.

"Oh, Merkley must have arrived," Sondra said, smiling wanly. "Who else could sound that starved. Come on, let's start our own party."

Sondra led them to a long table spread with delicacies. Peter noticed that whenever he took a slice of chicken, or ham, or some lobster salad, a waiter whisked the platter away and filled it up again.

They were all so busy enjoying the food that they paid no attention to Little Red Riding Hood, who had joined the group at the table. Unlike the rest of them, she did not remove her mask to eat. Instead, she poked the food in behind it.

Peter ate until he could hold no more. "Nice party," he said to Sondra as he put his mask back on.

"Thanks. But—Oh well, let's face it. It really isn't so hot. It'll be better when the show starts. Maybe all of them"— she gestured toward the wild crowd—"will sit down."

A gong sounded and there was a scramble for seats. Peter looked for Nick Vhartok, but couldn't pick him out in the crowded room.

The lights dimmed, and Peter saw what he knew must be Vhartok's dark form hunched in his usual chair by the stage. Something about Vhartok's costume made Peter strain to get a better look. Was it—

Peter waited until the entertainment started before he made his move. First he had to lose the short guy in the skeleton costume who had been shadowing him all evening.. He was sure now that he was one of Vhartok's men.

Peter darted this way and that between the chairs. He went on deck, then came back to the lounge, walking between two stewards. He ducked behind the long table of food and waited, crouching low. When he stood up and looked around, the short man in the skeleton costume was nowhere in sight—his strategy had worked. Now, if Vhartok acted as he had at the first party on the *Golden Goose*, Peter's plan might work.

He was not disappointed. As before, Vhartok rose from his chair, left the lounge, and immediately returned.

Carefully, Peter worked his way across the lounge. As he neared Nick Vhartok's chair, he deliberately stumbled.

In the confusion that followed, he pushed Vhartok's mask to one side.

"Hey, buddy, watch it!" a panda-bear bodyguard growled, jumping to his feet. His hoarse, menacing voice was no match for his innocent-looking costume.

Peter danced a few steps and bowed. He hoped they would think he was one of the tourists from the cruise ship.

Going out on deck, he stood by the rail. He needed time to think, for he had discovered something that shook him.

The man sitting in Vhartok's chair was not Nick Vhartok. When Peter had pushed the mask aside, he was astounded to feel beneath his fingers a head of thick, wiry hair.

There was only one reason for Nick Vhartok's using a double to fool his guests into thinking he was in the lounge when he was not. He needed an alibi. He was crafty enough to know he might be questioned about his shady dealings, so he had constructed the perfect cover-up. His guests—all respectable people—would swear he had not left the lounge during the whole evening.

Peter knew he was on to something big—he had to know more. And he counted on his costume to get him where he wanted to go. When he had uncovered Vhartok's double, he had also verified something he had suspected earlier— Nick Vhartok and his double were, like Peter, dressed as Moko Jumbie.

Peter entered the guarded passageway, and this time he was not stopped. A heavyset man dressed as Peter Rabbit said, "Evening, boss," and waved him by with a rubber carrot.

Peter followed the passageway to the metal steps and

85

down to the room below. The heavy door was ajar and he heard voices.

He remembered how that thick door had almost locked him in when he had wandered down there during the first party. But this time he was prepared. He took a wad of putty from his pocket and crammed it into the lock opening.

Drawing back quickly, he hid below the stairway. Two men came out of the room. They closed the door and climbed the stairs.

Peter's heart pounded. It was now or never.

He went to the door and turned the handle—slowly, slowly. For an awful second, it stuck. Then the door swung open. The putty had done the job and kept the lock from springing.

Peter entered the room, eased the door shut, and switched on the light. Bamboo crates were everywhere. Several had been broken open.

He took off his mask to see better. The contents of the crates—square packages wrapped in oil silk—were stacked on the floor. Peter rubbed his hand over the smooth material. It was a long shot, but maybe— No, he was sure. They were identical to the ones in the cave at Little Skull. Vhartok was using the little island as a transfer point.

But for what?

He worked at the seal on one of the packages until he could slip his fingers inside. He pulled out an oblong piece of paper. A quick glance told him it was money—a ten-dollar bill.

He reached into the package and pulled out another. And another.

Footsteps echoed on the metal stairs. Peter jumped for the light switch, clicked it off, and hid behind a bamboo crate. He held his breath as the footsteps passed by and receded down the passageway.

He was stretching his luck. He'd better get out of there. He opened the door a crack. All clear. He slipped out of the room and up the stairs to the deck. Only then did he realize that he had three ten-dollar bills in his hand. He had never stolen anything before. He would have to find some way to return the money.

When Peter entered the lounge, the show was going strong.

Lord Obnoxious was singing witty songs about people in the audience. The crowd roared at each clever verse.

The calypso singer finished his act and the spotlight shifted from him to the doorway by the stage. A waiter wheeled in a cart bearing a ten-layer birthday cake. The frosted tiers of pink and white were ablaze with candles.

"Oh, Uncle Nicky," Sondra squealed, "you didn't forget after all!" She ran to pull her uncle from his chair, but the man costumed as Moko Jumbie refused to move.

He shook her hand loose and stalked out. A moment later, Nick Vhartok—the real Nick Vhartok, Peter realized—came into the lounge. He had changed from his costume to a dark suit.

"What's the matter, Uncle Nicky?" Sondra asked. "Don't you want to help me cut my cake?"

"Sure, kid." Vhartok smiled stiffly and gave his niece an awkward little pat on the shoulder. "Gimme a knife, Bugsy," he commanded, and instantly a panda bear handed him a knife. Vhartok stepped backward and flourished the knife over the cake.

He was unaware of Little Red Riding Hood, who stood behind him, her eyes burning through the holes in her mask as she stared at the elaborate cake. Vhartok tripped over Red Riding Hood's foot, stumbled backward, and knocked her off-balance. She grabbed for his waist as his feet shot out from under him, upsetting the cart, cake and all.

Peter couldn't believe his eyes. There on the polished floor was Nick Vhartok—in Little Red Riding Hood's lap.

And in Vhartok's lap—the birthday cake. Some of the candles still flickered, those that had not been snuffed out when the pink and white frosting squashed against him, smearing his black suit. There was frosting on his black suede shoes too.

Vhartok brushed aside all offers of help and got to his feet. He whirled around, slipped on a glob of frosting, and went down, this time smashing what was left of the cake into a sodden mass.

His bodyguards rushed to the rescue. "Whaddayuh want we should do, boss?" one of them asked. This was the first time they had ever had to protect their boss from a birthday cake.

Little Red Riding Hood lay crumpled on the floor.

"Can I help you, ma'am?" Peter asked.

"Sure, Sonny-boy," she said.

Vhartok had not left the lounge, but stood by the door, watching Peter help the woman to her feet. She pushed her wig back into place. But she pushed too hard, and the curly blond wig and pink mask fell to the floor. It was Merkley Peach.

Vhartok's face froze. "Get out of here!" he exploded.

They had all been laughing at Merkley's clever disguise when the ugly words sliced through the air. The room fell silent.

"Get out! Get out!" he yelled. "All of yuh. Get out!"

Sondra turned her stricken eyes to Peter. But what could he do? She ran from the lounge sobbing.

The guests hurried off the yacht and onto the launch. Peter glanced around to see if the stubby guy in the skeleton suit had caught up with him. He was nowhere in sight. Vhartok had probably called off his men.

Peter's spirits were low. The party had ended miserably. And to make matters worse, he still didn't know what Vhartok was up to.

Suddenly he remembered the ten-dollar bills in his pocket. He handed them to Alexie, who stood quietly beside him on the launch.

"These belong there," he said, pointing toward the yacht.

The strings of lights that had outlined the ship were being switched off, row by row.

"What do you mean?" she asked.

"Oh, nothing. Just give this money to Sondra next time you see her. Tell her it belongs to her uncle. I got it by mistake."

"Oh," Alexie said, putting the bills in her purse.

Peter was glad to be rid of the ten-dollar bills. Whatever Vhartok's racket was, he was being paid a lot for it—crates of the stuff. Peter wanted no part of that kind of money.

9

Jake 'n' Steve do . . .

Jake 'n' Steve do gotta find it right
Last day now, dey gonna fly 'way tonight
Peter tell'm where to search in d'sea
An' what dey fisheen up you won' hear from me

THE MORNING after the party, the alarm jarred Peter
awake at five A.M. Jumping out of bed, he pulled on his
cutoff jeans. He moved quietly—no sense waking Jens and
having to answer a lot of questions. He could see the outline of his little brother's body curled up under the sheet.

It was still dark when he left the house.

As planned the afternoon before, he met Jake and Steve
in Frenchtown. At sunrise, they set off for Little Skull island
in the *Cha-Cha-Chug*.

"What do you think we'll find?" Peter asked.

"Hard to say," Jake replied. "Of course we know one
thing. Sea worms will have eaten the St. Francis image.
There'll be nothing left of it."

"That's one thing I don't understand," Peter said.

"What?"

"Why would El Sangre take a wooden statue?"

90

"Didn't we tell you about that?" Steve said.

"No."

"Well, we'd better fill you in. Father Fernando's letter reveals El Sangre's motive for stealing the statue. The priest was at his prayers when the pirates broke into the church. He barely had time to slip off the heavy ring he wore—his seal ring—and hide it in a small bronze casket, or box. The casket was made to fit into a secret compartment in the back of the St. Francis statue. When the door to the compartment was closed and locked, you would never suspect it was there.

"As I was saying, Father Fernando barely had time to hide his ring. Also in the bronze casket was all the money he had saved toward the building of a permanent church."

Steve leafed through the papers in his briefcase and pulled one out. "I'll translate the Father's letter for you.

"I was bent in prayer when I heard the sound of drunken laughter outside my door. Being forewarned of pirates hereabouts, I hurried to conceal my valuables. I scarce had hidden my ring in the niche of St. Francis when men burst in.

"Never have I seen such cruel, terrifying visages. They demanded my gold. I refused, and they snatched up the silver chalice and gold crucifix. They desecrated the sacred altar, laughing like demons.

"They put me to the sword. Though bleeding from my wounds, still I refused them my gold. One of the pirate crew, whom I adjudged the captain, spoke an order to his men. Thereupon, they took up the blessed image of St. Francis.

91

"I warned the captain to spare St. Francis, lest a dreadful fate befall his ship. Never have I seen a man such as he. His face bore a hideous scar running the full length of its left side. His eyes glistened with an unnatural light. Surely he was possessed of the devil.

"He ignored my warning and with a bitter laugh said, 'A lesson to all who would resist El Sangre! I take your foolish image. You will never see it again.'

"I watched helplessly as his men carried out the holy St. Francis. They did not know that the gold they sought was locked inside the blessed statue."

"You mean the pirates stole the gold without knowing it?" Peter asked.

"It sure looks that way," Steve replied. He returned the paper to his briefcase and pulled out another—the map Peter had made.

"We're almost there," Jake said, pointing to the outline of Little Skull.

They followed Peter's map to the spot where he had been swimming the day before.

"If I have it figured right," Peter said, "the wreck should be about here."

They anchored the boat. Jake and Steve strapped on their aqualungs. Peter was to stay in the boat and tend the lines. They had worked out a signal system: two jerks—pull up the bucket; one jerk—feed out more line.

Jake and Steve went over the side and disappeared into the water, streaming tiny bubbles behind them.

Peter waited. The time passed slowly, and he found himself wondering about Nick Vhartok's crates of money. He had told Jake and Steve of Vhartok's accident with the birthday cake. They had laughed and accused him of making it up. He had not told them about the bamboo crates or the man in the yellow pants.

The line jerked twice.

Peter grabbed the rope and hauled the bucket up. It was so heavy that he was puffing when he got it aboard. After he had emptied it and sent it down again, he studied the things piled at his feet. There were some broken bits of coral and a piece of iron shaped like a rib. But what was this? He turned a coral-encrusted object over and over in his hand. It was just about the right size for—yes, that was it— a pistol. It must have belonged to the pirates. Jake and Steve had found the wreck!

They worked all morning and into the afternoon without stopping. They dared not delay; Jake and Steve were leaving on the evening plane. Whatever they were going to find had to be found today.

In midafternoon, Peter hauled the bucket up for what seemed like the hundredth time. It was so heavy that he could barely get it out of the water. Bracing his feet against the side of the boat, he pulled with all his strength.

"Keep at it, Pete," a voice called out. Jake had come to the surface to help with the heavy load.

Together they got the bucket aboard. When Peter saw the letters on the metal object, he let out a whoop.

It was the bell.

Jake adjusted his breathing tube and jumped back into the water. In a few minutes, Peter felt a single jerk on the line. He fed out more line, and then more. They were going farther out.

A double jerk shook his hand, and Peter pulled the line in as fast as he could. When the bucket reached the boat it was empty. Jake and Steve must have abandoned the search.

What a shame to give up now, Peter thought as he looked out over the water. He blinked. Something broke the surface and appeared to ride the gentle waves. He could hardly believe his eyes, but there it was—a gold cross, Father Fernando's cross.

Jake's head popped into sight, and Peter realized that his friend was holding the cross in his hand. Steve followed close behind, and the two climbed into the boat.

"I think we've picked it clean," Jake said, unstrapping his heavy air tanks.

Steve carried a small box in his hand. "We didn't expect to find everything," he said. "I'm sorry we couldn't locate the silver chalice, though. Probably it was swept away long ago."

"Well, we've got the cross," Jake said, raising the treasure to admire it. "It was wedged underneath some heavy pieces of iron."

"We had to hack this out of a chunk of coral." Steve held up the small box. "It could be Father Fernando's bronze casket. We'll know when we get it open."

"What are we waiting for?" Jake said, tossing Steve his jackknife.

"Sure, mon, let's see what's in that box," Peter added eagerly.

He and Jake watched Steve carefully chip at the crust of coral with no luck. Finally he shrugged his shoulders. "O.K., Pete. Your turn."

94

Peter reached for the knife. He tried to pry it under the lid, but it was no use.

"Don't worry, Pete," Jake grinned. "It won't be long before we find out what's in the box." He flopped down on the sand and closed his eyes.

Steve set to work packing. He wrapped the heavy bell in a piece of canvas. He rolled the cross, the small chest, and the pistol in towels and placed them in duffle bags.

"Some job we had getting that stuff out," he said to Peter. "I'll bet we moved a ton of debris. I've never worked so hard in my life."

"But it was worth it," Peter smiled.

Steve looked at his watch. He and Jake were flying to Miami on the seven-forty plane. "Hey, Jake, wake up!"

They dropped Peter off in front of his house.

"You'll hear from us," Steve said.

"That's a promise," Jake added.

Peter knew they would keep their word. He ran up the steps to the house. Now he could tell his mother and father and Grandpa Van about the treasure hunt. And wait until Jens heard!

His mother met him at the door. "Isn't Jens with you?" she asked, looking worried.

"No, Mom. I left early this morning. He wasn't up yet."

"I don't understand," she said. "He hasn't been home all day. Not even to feed his cat."

"But he was still in bed when I left this morning, Mom."

They went up to the bedroom. Jens's form was curled up on his bed.

"Jens!" Peter called out, pulling the sheet away.

96

It was only a dummy made of pillows.

"Now why would he do that?" said Mrs. Van Dyke.

Peter searched the room for a clue. What he found hit him so hard he felt sick.

"Mom!"

"What?"

He pointed to a bare spot on the wall over the dresser. The skeleton mask and suit had been removed.

"Did Jens tell you anything before he went to bed, Mom?" Peter asked.

"Oh, you know him. Last night he was complaining that you've been away so much lately. He said the very next place you went, he was going too. I assumed he meant out with you today."

Peter's head whirled. The short guy at the party—the one in the skeleton costume who had followed him around —Jens!

"He's on the boat, Mom. He didn't come back with the rest of us. I've got to get him off!" Peter ran out of the house.

"Peter!" Mrs. Van Dyke cried. "Where?"

"On Nick Vhartok's yacht," Peter yelled as he flew down the steps. "Call the police!"

10

Jens caught in trap . . .

Jens caught in trap, he know too much
Peter gonna yank he from d'lion clutch
D'lion he have claw like knife
Watch out Peter or you lose your life

PETER ran until his side ached. When he got to the waterfront he was relieved to see the *Golden Goose* still riding at anchor in the harbor.

He looked anxiously up the street. Where were the police? Asleep, probably. He knew that bunch—they didn't know how to hurry! It'd be too late by the time they got going. He had to get on that boat—now!

He turned and ran toward Frenchtown. Glancing back as he ran, he saw Alexie pedaling furiously after him. She caught up with him on her bicycle.

"Wait, Peter!" she cried. "I want to show you something."

"Can't talk now," he panted, but he had to stop running to catch his wind.

"You have to. It's, it's—look!" She thrust three ten-dollar bills into his hand.

"What's this for?"

"It's the money you gave me. Remember? You said it was Vhartok's. I was supposed to give it to Sondra. But I didn't."

"What? Look, Alexie, I can't talk now. Vhartok's got Jens on his yacht. Jens sneaked into the party last night, and he hasn't been seen since."

"Oh, no!" Alexie moaned. "Now you've got to listen. Those ten-dollar bills are counterfeit."

"What? Are you sure?"

"Yes. I studied them under the microscope at the drugstore. Daddy checked them too. They're phony. I thought something fishy was going on. Sondra told me Vhartok sent her to her cabin a lot because he didn't want her snooping into his business deals."

"I've got to get Jens off that yacht."

"How are you going to get out there?"

"Uncle Pierre's boat."

"Hop on. We can get there faster on my bike."

They raced for Frenchtown, found the *Cha-Cha-Chug* moored in its usual place, and pushed off for the yacht.

"We'd better not go any closer," Peter said when they were a short distance from the *Golden Goose*. "I'll swim from here." He slipped over the side away from the yacht.

"Wait," Alexie warned.

A man appeared on the deck of the yacht near the gangway. He watched Alexie as she switched off the motor, took up a fishing rod and began casting.

"Good act," Peter said. He hung on to the side of the boat, staying low in the water so he could not be seen from the yacht. "He's one of Vhartok's bodyguards. I'm going to swim underwater. If the guard goes away, start the motor so I'll know the coast is clear."

"Where should I wait for you?" Alexie asked.

"Go over there," Peter said, pointing to a buoy a hundred yards away. "Keep the motor running. When you see Jens and me hit the water, get to us as fast as you can."

Peter ducked under and swam for the yacht. It was farther than he had thought, and he was forced to surface for air. But he had a trick of taking a breath with his face barely breaking the surface. The guard didn't notice the slight ripple he made.

He swam under the gangway and treaded water until Alexie started the *Cha-Cha-Chug*. The way was clear.

He pulled himself onto the lowest step of the gangway and crept up. Once on deck, he crouched low and hurried for cover.

He saw a stack of deck chairs and squeezed into the narrow space behind them. Now for—

"Peter?" a voice called softly.

He jumped. It was Sondra. She had seen him board.

"Thank heavens you're here," she said in a low voice. "They've got Jens."

"I know. Where is he?"

"I'm sure he's in cabin A," she said, pointing toward the starboard cabin. "They won't let me near there."

"Sondra, can I trust you?"

"Oh, yes," she replied. "You know about Uncle Nicky, don't you?"

"You mean his phony money?"

"Yes. I just found out, but he doesn't know I'm wise. I thought something crazy was going on when he had one of his men dress up to look like him and take his place at parties."

"I did too," Peter said.

"It didn't make sense," Sondra whispered, "until this morning when I overheard him talking to a man about a load of supplies. They had an awful argument about how much money the other man was to get. Then there was a crash, and I peeked around the corner. Peter—money was flying every which way! You never saw so much in your life. But you know what they did? They just kicked it into a pile."

"Well, that proves it. They wouldn't treat real money like that."

"It sure does," Sondra agreed. "And there's more. A foreign ship drops crates of money in a cave somewhere in the islands. I don't know where. Anyway, Uncle Nicky's man—he's called Whitey—goes to this cave and gets the crates. He takes them to St. Thomas and keeps them there —they have a secret storage room—until Uncle Nicky sends for food and stuff. Then they mix the crates in with the other packages. It really must be something big for them to go to all that trouble."

"Sondra, does this Whitey fellow wear yellow—" Peter began, but a deep, throbbing sound stopped him.

"The engines!" Sondra gasped. "Uncle Nicky said we were getting out of St. Thomas before dark."

"Sondra, you've got to help me."

"How?"

"Can you keep the *Golden Goose* from getting away?"

"I don't know," she answered, her voice shaking, "but I'll try."

"I'm going after Jens. Do something, Sondra! Don't let this yacht get out of the harbor!"

Peter crept along the deck to cabin A. He crouched under a partly opened porthole. Someone was talking.

"Listen, kid," a familiar voice growled, "I've treated you nice, huh? Gave you candy 'n' ice cream. But you ain't gettin' more until you spill it. Who put you onto me?"

Peter shuddered. It was Nick Vhartok.

"I told you already. Nobody sent me," came the reply. Peter recognized Jens's voice. "Why won't you tell me how come you have all those million suits. My daddy only has two."

"Don't you know nothin' but questions? Sheddup the smart stuff, kid, or I'll let you have it."

"Have what?" Jens piped. "More ice cream?"

"I'm gonna give you one last chance, kid. Now tell me, who paid you to sneak on board?"

"Nobody paid me. I don't even get a 'lowance at home. Daddy says I don't know the valor of money."

"See if you understand this!"

The sound cracked through the air like a whip.

Vhartok had slapped Jens. Peter could hear his brother whimpering and bit his lip to control his anger. An outburst now would be fatal.

A door slammed. Silence.

Peter edged closer to the porthole and tried to look in through the crack. But all he could see was the back of a chair.

How could he get Jens's attention? He couldn't risk calling out. What could he do? *The code!*

S-O-S, Peter tapped on the glass. P-E-T-E-R H-E-R-E S-O-S.

Jens's frightened eyes appeared in the crack.

"Open it," Peter whispered.

Jens unhooked the chain and opened the porthole. "Am I ever glad to see you!" he whispered.

"Can you get out the cabin door?" Peter asked.

"No. There's a guy standing outside."

Peter gauged the porthole opening. His plan might work. It was their only chance.

"Take off your shirt," he whispered to Jens.

Jens looked puzzled, but quickly obeyed.

"Now hold out your arms."

Peter tried to pull Jens through the porthole, but was stopped when the top of Jens's pants caught on the inside.

Jens dropped back into the cabin.

"Off," he said, popping up again.

They tried once more, but still Jens's round body would not slip through the opening. Back he went.

Peter looked through the porthole into Vhartok's cabin, at a loss as to what to do next. His own reflection stared back at him from a large mirror above the dresser. A row of jars caught his eye.

"Jens, bring me a couple of those jars."

Jens tiptoed across the cabin, took the two largest jars, and brought them to Peter.

Peter read the label on the first one: MAGIC HAIR RE-STORER. He uncapped it. It was half full of a sickly sweet, runny liquid. "This won't do," he said, handing the jar back to Jens. The second one was labeled MIRACLE BALD-NESS PREVENTATIVE. Peter opened it. It was filled with a thick cream, just what they needed.

"Rub this all over. Especially there," Peter told Jens, pointing to his stomach.

Jens looked surprised, but obeyed without a word. When he was coated with the cream, he climbed the chair and stood by the porthole. Peter grasped him by the arms and pulled. Jens popped through the porthole like a cork shot out of a bottle.

"Now hang on to me tight," Peter said. He grabbed his brother under the arms and jumped overboard.

Someone cried out. They had been seen.

Jens clung to Peter's jeans as they swam. Like fish, they flashed through the water below the surface. But they had to come up to gulp air. The water around them hissed and spat as bullets hailed down.

Suddenly the shooting stopped. A cruise ship was approaching. Using the big ship for cover, Jens and Peter struck out to meet the *Cha-Cha-Chug,* which was bearing down on them at top speed.

Alexie helped them into the boat and sped toward the waterfront. Peter and Jens lay in the bottom, panting. Jens still had his hand clamped onto the top of Peter's jeans.

"Pretty lucky pants," Peter said when he got his breath.

Alexie threw Jens a ragged shirt she found under the seat. "Here," she said, "you can put this on."

Jens wrapped the shirt around his middle and tied the sleeves together to hold it up.

Peter looked back at the *Golden Goose.* What would happen to Sondra? He felt terrible leaving her to fend for herself until the police could get on the job.

"Look!" he shouted, pointing to the *Golden Goose.*

104

The yacht had veered sharply off its seaward course.

"If it keeps going that way, it'll run ashore," Alexie said. "I wonder who's at the wheel."

Torrential rain pelted the windows of the Van Dyke living room. Peter lay on the couch reading. He knew what was coming when Jens brought the big glossy magazine and put it on his stomach.

"Read it again?" Jens begged.

"You can read, Jens," Peter protested.

"But I want you to read it. 'Specially the part about Ottilie Opal."

"Well, O.K.," Peter sighed. He put his book down and sat up.

Jens curled in a chair with his cat, Beauty, clinging to his shoulder. Since Jens's return, the cat had become his adoring slave. Jens could go nowhere without Beauty tagging along.

Peter opened the magazine and read, " 'Island Boys Cook Nick Vhartok's Golden Goose.' "

"I like that!"

"Aren't you sick of this?" Peter asked. "You've heard it over and over for a week."

"Yeah, I know. But I like it anyway. Read me the part about Ottilie Opal."

Peter continued, " 'Ottilie Opal Fetching, . . .' "

"Her initials spell Oo-oof!" Jens giggled.

" '. . . who goes by the name of Sondra Fetching, grounded the yacht *Golden Goose* after incapacitating the captain.' "

"Pass-a-tating. I forgot what that means," Jens said.

"It means she knocked him out. You remember." Peter read on, " 'Sondra used the only weapon she could lay her hands on in a hurry. She grabbed a fire extinguisher from the wall near the steering wheel, aimed it at the captain's head—and sprayed.' "

Jens knew the story by heart, but he listened wide-eyed. "Go on. Read the rest."

" 'According to Miss Fetching, the captain whirled around and struck her in the face. The extinguisher crashed to the deck, and the captain tripped over it and fell. He was knocked unconscious.

" 'Sondra was found at the wheel, clinging for dear life. Her face was badly bruised, and at her feet lay the unconscious captain.' "

"Hold up the picture," Jens pleaded.

Peter sighed. There was no use fighting it. He had to go along with Jens until the excitement over the capture of Nick Vhartok died down. He held up the picture of Sondra, head bandaged, smiling, and holding up a fire extinguisher.

"Boy," Jens laughed, "she musta squirted him good!"

Mrs. Van Dyke came into the room with a handful of letters.

"More mail, Peter," she said, smiling.

Since the big photo magazine had sent a reporter and a photographer to St. Thomas to cover the capture of Nicholas Vhartok, leader of an international counterfeit ring, the letters had been pouring in. Some were from girls who wrote silly stuff. Peter let his mother answer those.

But he was tired of all the questions and letters and people who came to stare and point at his picture in their copy of the magazine. He would be glad when the next issue came out and it was all forgotten.

He had told the police everything. They had caught up with Vhartok's yacht shortly after Sondra ran it aground. But Nick Vhartok had almost slipped through their net. The police caught him just as he was about to leap from the gangway of the *Golden Goose* to the deck of a waiting motor launch.

"It were he stateside hat helpeen us," a policeman had told Peter. "If not, maybe we chaseen he clear to San Juan."

A gust of wind had caught the brim of Nick Vhartok's gray felt hat just as he was about to jump to the escape boat. He had grabbed for the hat and lost his balance.

"We fisheen he outa d'watah like a drown' mongoose," another policeman had said with a chuckle.

Enough evidence had been gathered against Nick Vhartok and his men to put them in jail for a long time. And Whitey Hawker, the man with the yellow pants and bandaged head, had been caught racing out of St. Thomas harbor in his motor launch. Whitey was trapped by his own greed. Not satisfied with his payoff, he had stolen a package of counterfeit bills. Police found the money hidden in his boat.

Sondra was staying with Alexie. When Mrs. Fetching heard of her daughter's heroism, she sent a wire saying she was flying to St. Thomas immediately. But she hadn't been heard from since. It had happened before, Sondra explained, so she wasn't surprised. Mrs. Fetching had a way of forgetting things.

Mrs. Du Bois insisted that Sondra make her home with them for as long as she liked. She told Sondra that she hoped she would go to school with Alexie in the fall.

"Aren't you going to read your letters?" Mrs. Van Dyke asked Peter.

"Oh, uh, sure," Peter said, flipping through the envelopes. Letters had come from all over the world, but the one he wanted most was not there. He had heard nothing from Jake and Steve since the day they had discovered the wreck of the *Ana Rosabella*.

"Is this all?" he asked.

"Oh, here's one I held out. I didn't want to get it mixed in with the others." She smiled as she watched him read the return address.

He ripped open the envelope and read eagerly:

Dear Pete,

It looks like you turned out to be a big hero. But we know it hasn't gone to your head—ha, ha.

You must be anxious to hear about the things we found at Little Skull. Well, we finally got the box open and guess what? It contained Father Fernando's small store of gold coins and his seal ring! This was the ring he told about hiding in the St. Francis statue in the letter we read to you. We couldn't believe our good luck. But without you, we wouldn't have had a chance.

Since we know you wouldn't take a cent for helping us (even though you worked pretty darn hard) we have played a trick on you. We "borrowed" some of your paintings and showed them to a friend of ours who runs an art school in New York. You will be hearing from him soon. He was so impressed with your pictures that he wants to see more. He said you show a lot of promise, and if you want to go to art school in a few years, to let him know.

Thanks again, Pete, for all the help you gave us. We'll never forget you, or the Virgin Islands.

Your friends,

Jake and Steve

Peter read the letter several times. Then he looked out the window. The tropical rainstorm had stopped as abruptly as it had started. "Does Dad need me at the shop today, Mom?" It was Mr. Van Dyke's first day at the shop since recovering from his illness.

"I don't think so, Peter. You know your father. He wants to show us that he's his old self again. Besides, Grandpa Van is there to help if he needs it."

"Then if it's O.K. with you, I think I'll go out to Coki Bay."

"Of course, Peter, go ahead. But don't forget to come home for supper."

Peter tucked his painting kit under his arm and walked into the warm Caribbean sun. He could hardly wait to get down to the sea. You never knew what you might find there.

This is end of story, my very good friends
So say good-by to Peter, Alexie, and Jens
Take my advice when you forget how to smile
Jus' hop a little boat an' sail to Virgin Isle

West Indian Terms

Calypso talk
West Indian jargon

Cha-Cha hat
a tall hat made of palm fronds, and often decorated with straw flowers, donkeys, etc. A style originated in Frenchtown.

continental
person born on one of the continents

freebs
Calypso for something free, a handout

gade
street (Danish)

Go-Down Day
an imaginary holiday. Virgin Islanders love holidays and declare one at the slightest excuse.

grape tree
tropical tree bearing sea grapes. It grows near the shore, to a maximum of fifteen feet.

Island White
a Virgin Island expression for someone who appears white, but has Negro blood

Jumbie
a West Indian ghost

Kronprindsens Gade
Crown Prince's Street

Little Skull
a small, imaginary island, typical of hundreds surrounding St. Thomas

mammee
a fruit with a leathery, brown skin. The three seeds inside the mammee fruit often give mammees a skull-like appearance.

mammeehead
a bald person

manchineel
a tree that grows on sandy beaches in many parts of the tropics. Its yellowish-green fruit is similar to crab apples, but is extremely poisonous.

Moko Jumbie
the Spirit of Carnival

sea egg
sea urchin

Sondra-birthday
Calypso for Sondra's birthday

stateside
a person or thing from the U.S.A.

U. S. Virgin Islands

St. Croix, largest of the three. Known for its gently rolling country and colonial sugar-cane plantations.

St. Thomas, liveliest and most densely populated.

St. John, smallest. Most of this island is now a United States National Park.

whelks
sea snails

whenyoureach?
Calypso for When did you get here?